THE ILLUSTRATED STORY-TELLER.

THE BRAVO'S SECRET.

LONDON: W. S. JOHNSON, 60, ST. MARTIN'S LANE, CHARING CROSS.

TO BE HAD OF ALL BOOKSELLERS.

The Illustrated } No. 19.
Story-Teller.

THE BRAVO'S SECRET.

FOUNDED ON INCIDENTS WHICH OCCURRED DURING THE LATTER PERIOD OF THE
REIGN OF FRANCISCO DANDOLO, DOGE OF VENICE.

CHAPTER I.

The origin of the "Council of Ten," and their peculiar duties—The midnight session—The chief spy—Niccoli, and his character—The private interview at the palace of the patrician Marino Trivisano.

NEAR the commencement of the fourteenth century, while Petro Gradenigo reigned as Doge of Venice, three nobles formed a plot for the overturn of the Venetian government; but before their scheme could be carried into execution, their designs were discovered, and though they fought bravely for nearly a whole day, yet they were conquered, and, after an investigation of the affair, most of the conspirators were allowed to leave the city. For the examination of this conspiracy, a commission, consisting of ten members of the senate, was appointed, whose term of office was limited to fourteen days, but afterwards the time was extended; and, after various prorogations, it was, during the reign of Francesco Dandolo, declared perpetual, under the name of the "Council of Ten," and it has since been one of the most important features in that government. The peculiar office of this council is to protect the people from the unjust exercise of power by the nobility, and also to protect the state from the influence of treason and faction; consequently, it is not regulated by any stated laws, but is subject only to its own judgment and the force of circumstances, and is, moreover, entirely independent of the senate. In order to carry out their plans, the Ten employ, as their spies, a crowd of monks, common prostitutes, gondoliers, and lackeys, who are scattered all over Venice and its dependencies; so that even the most confidential servant of a noble may be a spy upon his master's actions, ready to convey the intelligence of the slightest appearance of treason to the dreaded council.

The dark mantle of night had been for several hours spread over the city of Venice, and, though midnight was near at hand, still the Council of Ten was in session, awaiting the arrival of one of its most busy spies. Just as the bells of St. Mark tolled the hour of twelve, the Ten were relieved of their anxiety by the secret signal of the expected messenger, and the next moment he was ushered into their presence.

"Well, Niccoli," said the chief of the council, "what news do you bring us of this bravo?"

"If you mean Martelino," replied the spy, "I can give you but little information."

"I do mean Martelino. Did you not see him?"

"Yes," answered the spy, "I saw him at one of the casinos over beyond San Paolo; and I used every means in my power to get at his character, and also to ascertain where he came from, but it was of no use, for he seemed to mistrust in a moment what my intentions were, and he gave such answers, that I was completely baffled. Of one thing, however, I am sure—he is engaged in some business which he desires to keep secret, but whether it concerns only himself, or whether it is aimed against the state, is more than I have yet been able to discover."

"And what of the patrician Trivisano—have you seen him?" asked the chief.

"No, I have not seen him; but I have two trusty spies in his own household, and we shall be sure to hear of his movements."

"Well," said the chief, as he rolled up a small bundle of parchments, and placed it in his bosom, "I had hoped to have learned more of this Bravo, but as it is, we must wait for further developments. Let all the courtezans whom you can trust be set upon his track, and be sure that he does not leave Venice."

"But why not arrest him and bring him before the council at once?" suggested Niccoli.

"Because," answered the chief, "that would spoil the whole; for we have reason to suspect that he is engaged in some conspiracy, and, in order to get at the secret, we must move cautiously."

"Very well," returned the spy, "I will do all I can, and you shall learn the result of my efforts."

As Niccoli closed, he made a respectful bow to the councillors, and withdrew from the chamber; soon after which the council broke up, but with the understanding that they were to meet again on the following night.

As Niccoli stepped from the council chamber into the street, he drew his cloak up around the lower part of his face, and started off at a quick walk. He was a powerful-built man, with a countenance upon which one might gaze for a long time without arriving at any definite conclusions concerning his true character; for there was a peculiar expression of secret cunning about his quick, sharp eye and compressed lip, that would baffle the keenest observer of human nature, from the very fact that those lineaments, by which one would seek to read his character, were ever changing in their signs and tokens. From forty to fifty years must have passed over his head; but his exact age was as uncertain as his character. He had been the chief spy of the Council of Ten for about five years, and to him was entrusted the duties not only of looking after suspicious characters, but also the power of establishing the means of espionage wherever he thought proper. To the council he was a most valuable servant, for during the time he had served them but one single individual whom he sought had escaped him. Not a cabal could exist, nor a secret meeting of any kind take place, but their whole proceedings were known to the dreaded Niccoli. No one knew how nor where he gained his intelligence, only they knew that all their plans were sure to be discovered. One man, however, had baffled all his ingenuity—Marco Martelino, the bravo, always escaped him, and still he knew that this same bravo was engaged in nearly all the plots which he had discovered, for Martelino made no secret of his daring movements.

Niccoli walked on till he reached the palace of the patrician Marino Trivisano, where he stopped; and after looking cautiously round to see that he was not observed, he noiselessly approached a small latticed door, which he opened with a key of his own, and entered the building. The way which he took seemed to be a sort of secret passage; and after threading several intricate windings, he entered a small apartment at a remote angle of the building, within which sat a man engaged in carving a wooden model from a small key, which ever and anon he compared with the work before him.

"Ah, Niccoli!" exclaimed the workman, as the spy entered.

"—sh! not so loud, Pascal. I would not have that name heard within these walls by any ear save your own," said Niccoli, as he carefully secured the door by which he had entered.

"Oh, you need not fear, for there is no one in this part of the building save ourselves."

"Never mind that," quietly replied the spy; "there are walls very near to us, and you know not how many ears a wall may hide. When you have been exposed to danger as long as I have, you will learn to fear even a stone when you would reveal a secret. The lord Trivisano must not know that I have ever been in this place."

"He will never gain that information from any indiscretion of mine, you may depend."

"I believe you, Pascal, and all I would urge upon you is caution. But now to business. In the first place, when can you let me have the keys?"

"That is more than I can tell," replied Pascal Modetti, as he held up the wooden model upon which he had been at work. "This is the first one, and you know there are five more, and I can only work at them after my lord has retired; and even then I must run my risk of getting them."

"Very well," said Niccoli, taking up the model, and examining it; "just do them as soon as possible—I can expect no more. But now, what of Martelino, has he been here to-night?"

"I think he has. At any rate, there has been a man conversing with my master who answers very well to the description I have heard of him."

"Was he a large, powerfully-built man?" asked the spy.

"Yes," answered Pascal.

"Did he have a little stoop in his gait?"

"Yes."

"And was he slightly humped upon the back?"

"Exactly."

"Did he sit forward, and rest his hand upon his knees, when he conversed?"

"Yes."

"Did you get a glimpse at his face?"

"Yes, and an uglier-looking set of features I never saw."

"That is the man," replied Niccoli, while a peculiar smile rested upon his lips, called up by the earnestness of his companion's last remark. "But did you hear their conversation?"

"Not much of it," answered Pascal; "but I heard enough to know that they are both of them engaged in some plot against the state, and that there are others beside them who are also engaged in it."

"So far, so good. Now, Pascal, this is something which you will not mention to a living soul. You understand it."

"Yes," replied Pascal, while a slight trembling, which he could not suppress, seized his limbs, as he saw the keen eyes of the spy fixed upon him.

"There is one other thing which I desire that you should do for me," continued Niccoli, "and that is, to find out how many of the other servants are particularly attached to their master."

"Oh, as to that, I can tell you now. Over half of them dislike him altogether, and were it not that all the good places in Venice are already filled, they would not stay with him another week."

"Then I must trust you with an important duty, but it is one which you can easily perform, if you are careful. I want six good, trusty servants to be set upon the watch, so that you can get such information from them as you may desire; and it may be that they will be needed for something more important, ere long. Do you think you can do it?"

"I know I can," confidently replied Pascal.

"Then," said Niccoli, as he rose to go, "I shall leave the matter in your hands, and I trust that you will exercise all the discrimination you are master of in the work."

Pascal Modetti promised to do his best, and the spy of the Ten seemed satisfied with the result of the interview.

As Niccoli stepped upon the pavement in front of Trivisano's palazzo, a very close observer might have seen a tear glisten in his eye, but it was gone in a moment, and as he strode off into the darkness he murmured:—

"Oh, Venice, I love thee as a mother, and I swear to protect thee so long as there is one drop of blood in my veins!"

CHAPTER II.

Alberte Lioni—His present situation, and the cause of it—A picture—The storm, and the two gondolas—The lightning, and its fearful effects—Alberte's heroic conduct, and its results.

ON the evening succeeding the interview of the spy and Pascal Modetti, a small gondola put off from a spot near the Rialto, and smoothly glided down the Grand Canal towards the long row of splendid palaces which flanked the water, raising their marble walls over the moon-lit stream, and reflecting the bright beams of the full moon upon the gently rippling surface, like silver glances from fairy eyes. The boat was propelled by a youth of not more than one-and-twenty summers, over whose whole form was thrown that peculiar grace and ease which never fails to arrest and enchain the attention, but his countenance was the most remarkable, for it presented a theme for deep study. There was none of that effeminacy which marks the votary of ease and pleasure, and which so many mistake for beauty; but though his face was pale and slightly haggard, still it was handsome in the extreme—handsome from the fact that there was something there to be loved besides mere physical beauty, something which told of a pure and lofty mind, something which spoke to the sympathizing heart of a soul that beamed with all the finest gleams of humanity. He was slightly built, but yet finely moulded; and as he dexterously shot his light craft along over the sparkling water, steering clear of the hundreds of gondolas that crowded the canal, he frequently met a nod of recognition, and many a fair damsel turned her head and strained her love-lit eyes to watch the handsome youth as he shot away out of sight.

Such was Alberte Lioni, one of the most promising young artists of Venice. Twelve years before, Giovanni Marcello, one of the most powerful nobles of Venice, had been arrested for treason, and the council sentenced him to perpetual banishment, together with his whole family, and ordered that the names and arms of the house of Marcello should be stricken from the patrician list. A few years after his banishment, the elder Marcello wrote to the senate, and asked that his son, Alberte, might be allowed to return to his native city, and pursue his studies. "Though God knows that I am innocent of the crime you have imputed to me, and perhaps He alone, yet you all know that my poor boy is innocent," wrote the banished noble; and so feelingly did he set forth his claims, that the council which had been formed since Marcello was banished, consented that the boy might come to Venice, but with the proviso that he should take some other name than that of his father's, and that he should never lay claim to patrician rank.

Under the name of Lioni, therefore, the young Alberte came to his native city, and as he easily found friends, he had no difficulty in pursuing his studies. The stately palace which had once been his father's, and where his own feet had trod out their childish gambols, was now in the possession of Marino Trivisano, and often, as he passed its marble front, would a tear start to his eye, while the thought of his poor father's sufferings came across his mind; but for himself he cared but little, for he had already marked out for himself a brilliant course of life, and he even now pictured in the future a laurel wreath of fame for the name of Lioni, more bright and lasting than the diamond of the ducal bonnet of Venice, or the mere bauble of pompous nobility.

When Alberte Lioni dreamed this dream, he little knew what strange desires a few years might bring to his soul.

The youth had been in Venice but three years, when he received the melancholy intelligence of his father's death, who had not been able to stand up under the severe shock he had received. Six years had he dragged out in a foreign land, and then the name of Marcello ceased to be spoken.

In the letter which he indited to his son just before his death, he wrote:—

"In a few short hours, Alberte, there will be none left to bear the name of my house. You are forced to bear another; but though people may only know you as Lioni, the young student, yet do not cease to remember that God knows you as the son of an honest man; and may you never tarnish that honor which all the councils and senates in Christendom cannot take from you. When your mother died, she uttered her last prayer for you, and I now do the same—God bless you, my son. Farewell!"

This was a sad blow to the youth, but with a firm resolution to perform his duties truly and faithfully, he pursued his onward course; and now, when he is introduced to the reader he has nearly reached the end of his studies and hopes soon to produce something of which he can be proud; but in doing this, he has well nigh undermined his health, as a look at his pale features will shew.

Alberte rowed on, and as the cool, refreshing breeze of evening swept soothingly across his somewhat fevered brow, he thought not of time nor distance, and ere he was aware of the fact, he had nearly reached the mouth of the canal, and a few more strokes would have carried him out into the Adriatic. As he rested upon his oars, his eyes wandered along the flashing waves until they rested upon a small cluster of islands which separate the laguna from the gulf, and which serve, in a great measure, to break the force of the Adriatic storms before they reach the city; and so intently was his attention fixed upon the scene, and so sweetly was his artist's soul drinking in the inspiration of the time and place, that he did not notice another gondola, which had approached near to where his own lay. While he yet sat gazing upon nature's fair picture, he was suddenly aroused by the strange stillness of the air, and as he looked around upon the dark surface of the waters, he found that the gentle ripples, which had but a few moments before been dancing merrily in the moon's bright beams, had now sunk into a smooth mirror, which was reflecting a darkening sky, while far away, over the domes and spires of Venice, were rising a mass of sable clouds, whose frowning summits already reached half-way to the zenith. As he quickly turned the head of his light craft back towards the city, he noticed the other gondola, and a slight shudder ran through his frame as he saw that it contained only two females.

"Back! back!" he shouted, as soon as he noticed them. "Back, for your lives!"

But there was no need for his warning, for, ere he spoke, the females' gondola was on the move, and Alberte found that their boat skipped over the water faster than his own.

The clouds grew thicker and rose faster, and ere many moments a light moaning, like the low growl of the forest monarch, broke upon the young man's ears, and the next instant the storm was upon them in all its ungovernable fury. Harder and harder did Alberte ply his oars, and louder sounded the blast; the breaking waves dashed over the bows of his boat, completely deluging him in their relentless flood, while the rain fell in an almost blinding torrent. Ever and anon did he look forward to catch a glimpse of the frail bark ahead, but the girls pulled nobly, and he saw that they were gradually distancing him.

At length, not more than fifteen minutes after the storm broke, a sheet of flame poured forth from the dark clouds, and as it danced in its fearful vividness over the canal, Alberte was for a few minutes completely blinded by its lurid power; but simultaneous with the roar of the dread thunder there came upon the young man's ears a shriek so sharp and piercing, that he forgot the shock he had just received, and leaping quickly up in his boat, he strained his eyes through the darkness to where he had last seen the gondola. His heart leaped with a quick bound, as another flash of lightning lit up the foam-lashed water, and revealed to his gaze the fearful work which had been wrought by the preceding heaven-sent bolt. There, about a cable's length ahead, he distinctly saw the two females clinging to two separate portions of their ill-fated gondola, which had been rent in twain by the fatal fluid, sending forth their fast-weakening cries for help. With a power which he never before knew himself to be possessed of, did he ply his short, stout oars, and in a few minutes he reached the one nearest to him, whom he grasped with a firm hold, while yet she was crying for help. As Alberte raised her to his boat, she cast one imploring glance upwards, which was revealed by the still lurid heavens, and murmuring, "Save my mistress! for God's sake, save my young mistress!" she fell back insensible to the dangers which had beset her.

Had Alberte lost another moment it would have been too late to finish his work of salvation, for as he turned he could just distinguish through the gloom a portion of the wreck and the flutter of a white garment, just beneath it, which was being swept past him by the angry wind. With a quick movement he seized a boat-hook which happened to lay above the thwarts, and was just in season to grasp the wreck, ere it was swept away for ever, while with another movement he caught the lashing of his signal-mast for support, and reaching as far out as possible, he was just able to lay hold upon the girl's garment, at the very moment when her weakened hold had left her only support, and with an almost superhuman effort—at least for one like him—he raised the insensible form of the drowning female into his boat.

Alberte Lioni once more grasped his oars, and for a few moments he pulled bravely up against the storm; but Nature had done her utmost in the fierce struggle which had passed, and the heroic youth felt that he could do no more. He felt his muscles beginning to relax; a mist was gathering before his eyes, through which even the vivid lightning failed to penetrate; his head grew dizzy, and his brain reeled in unison with the frail bark he would have forced onward. Once, and only once, after his arms refused their office, did Alberte feel sensible to anything about him; he felt that he must give up to the giant storm, that the lives he would have saved must, after all, be lost, and that his own, as well, must return to the God who gave it. Then came a shock, like the meeting of two surging bodies, and the next moment he felt himself borne away by some invisible power. One simple sentence trembled upon his lips: "Father—mother—I come to meet you!" and Alberte Lioni sank into the darkness of mental night.

CHAPTER III.

The stranger—The rescue—Marco Martelino, the Bravo of Venice—His interview with the senator, Francis Vivaldi, and the results thereof.

AT the time when the storm first broke, there was standing far down the bank of the canal, near the spot where the ill-fated gondola was destroyed, a large man, who seemed eagerly watching the progress of the two boats. His height was slightly over six feet, and his muscular frame was developed in proportion, while the only defect in his build was a slight stoop, and somewhat of a hump upon the top of his back; but even this gave to his stout frame a look of more than ordinary physical power, even for one so large as himself. On his head he wore a wide-rimmed sombrero, from the right of which waved a large black ostrich feather, while his face, catching the shade of the dark plume, looked almost as lowering as the storm itself. The rest of his dress, as we can make it out by the almost continuous stream of lightning, consisted of a dark frock, heavily fringed with yellow stuff, fastened around the waist by a leathern belt, from which was suspended, on the present occasion, a long Milan sword; buckskin tights covered his legs, and on his feet he wore a pair of light sandals.

When the gondola in which were the two females was rent in twain, the stranger uttered an exclamation of horror, betraying a very different feeling from what his appearance would seem to indicate, and with a quick bound he started for the nearest boat. This he found chained but with one sweep; of his mighty arms he tore the staple from its post, and in a moment more he was shooting away for the scene of disaster; but, ere he reached it, the two girls had been transferred to the gondola of Alberte Lioni.

The new comer, however, was just in season to grasp the young man as he was falling back upon his seat, and it was the work of but a few moments to place all three in his own boat. Then he plied his oars with a power that sent his bark up against the storm with remarkable speed, and ere long he neared the sumptuous palaces which flank the canal. As he drew towards the bridges, he discovered that there was a great commotion near the palace of the lord Vivaldi—that the gondolas were being put off in all directions, while hundreds of torches sent their lurid glow down the canal.

"Halloo!" shouted the boatman, as a number of the gondolas neared him. "Do you seek the lady Isidora?"

"Yes, yes," came from a hundred voices.

"Back, then, back, and don't block up the way, for I have her here."

In a moment the gondoliers pulled their boats out of the way, and with a dozen strokes of his oars the stranger shot his craft up to the foot of the staircase which led to the palace of Francis Vivaldi, and throwing the bow-fast to those on shore, he raised the insensible form of Isidora Vivaldi in his arms.

"Tell me, sir—for God's sake—tell me, is my child alive?" cried an old man who stood trembling upon the steps.

"Yes, Vivaldi," answered the stranger, "her heart still beats."

"Thank God for that," murmured the old noble, as he received the form of his daughter into his arms, and imprinted a kiss upon her cold brow.

"Let some give their help here, Vivaldi," continued the powerful boatman, "for here are two more who deserve your attention."

In a few moments the servant girl and Alberte Lioni were removed to the house, and all the attention which the best skill could suggest was bestowed upon them. Ere long they all showed signs of life; but, alas, for Alberte! when he opened his eyes, it was only with the wild stare of feverish delirium. His already weakened constitution had received a shock which set his sensitive nerves into a wild commotion, and the fire of a malignant fever rolled like molten lava through his veins. But he was in the hands of those who owed him much, and his couch was watched with the most assiduous attention.

"But for yourself, sir, what can I do for you?" asked the lord Vivaldi, as the stranger closed his tale of the noble manner in which the youth had saved the lady Isidora and her maid. "Had it not been for you, they must have all been lost, and the noble youth would have fallen a sacrifice to his own magnanimity."

"I wish for nothing further than you will remember the deed, and, when you next hear my dreaded name, you will know that one kind act at least rests upon my shoulders."

"But tell me who you are," uttered the noble, as he instinctively drew back a pace from his strange companion.

"I am one who, should the spies of the Ten see you in conversation with me, might bring harm upon your head."

"You are not—no, that cannot be; for you would never have dared to enter the house of the chief of the Criminal Tribunal."

"I am MARCO MARTELINO," returned the stranger, in a deep voice; "and I dare go anywhere, whithersoever it pleases me."

"You—the Bravo of Venice?—he who is mixed up in every plot that has been discovered for years?—who seems to sin on with perfect impunity, slipping through the fingers of justice at every turn, as though you possessed the power of rendering yourself invisible?—he who seems to be at the very foundation of every wicked deed in Venice?"

"Well," calmly replied the Bravo, as the old noble drew tremblingly back, "why might I not as well bear that name as to have its stigma fixed upon some one else? You tremble, sir; but look ye, Vivaldi, when you cast your eyes around your senate chamber to-morrow, thou shalt see more than one noble sitting there who shall yet tremble before the nod of Marco Martelino. You say I have plotted. Aye, I have plotted, and I will plot again; for there be those in Venice whom I would see removed from power; their presence here suits me not, and you, sir, would you rest in peace, attempt not to thwart me, for I tell thee, Francis Vivaldi—senator and chief though you be—that should you step between me and my designs, your life is not worth a beggar's mite. You will set spies upon my track in vain; for even your boasted Niccoli, who has seized upon every one else whom he has sought, has hunted after me to no purpose. At all the casinos in Venice he has his hundreds of spies, but they dare not betray me, or if they would, they cannot. At every ridotto and masquerade, your chief spy has his emissaries, but I go in and come out when I please; aye, and I plot there, too, if it suits me. Dost comprehend me, Vivaldi?"

The old noble made no answer, but he gazed upon the wonderful man before him with silent awe; nor could he repress a feeling somewhat akin to admiration, as he witnessed the proud bearing of the bravo; yet he was the man whom Venice most feared; and, though he stood now in his own house, within his very hall of state, the Senator Vivaldi thought not of attempting his capture. He trembled before his dark presence.

"Tell me," continued Martelino, as he saw that his companion did not speak, "can the laws of Venice make that which is absolutely *wrong* to be by any means *right?*"

"Of course not," replied Vivaldi, who thought he saw in the manner of the Bravo a disposition to reveal some portion of his designs.

"Then tell me, how shall our senators be corrected when they do wrong?"

"They are amenable to the Council of Ten," replied the noble.

"Ay, and so is the doge himself, and so is every one," said Martelino, while a peculiar fire flashed from his eyes. "But when your Ten do wrong, and your senate do wrong, and your inquisitors do wrong, what may we do then? From them there is no appeal. Wherever your Council of Ten sets its seal, there it must stay, and no power in Venice can remove it."

"If the senate do that which ought not to be done, and continue in the pursuance of the wrong, then the people must mend it."

"Ah, beware, Vivaldi, that smells of treason."

Vivaldi started at this remark, and as he caught the keen eye of the Bravo fixed upon him, a strange feeling of uneasiness crept over his soul. What it was, or from whence it sprung, he could not tell.

"Now," continued Martelino, "your councils have done wrong, and it must be made right. If the people protest, it is treason; if you, or I, or any one else, move among the people in this matter, we are the traitors, and death must be the consequence. So you see how slight a thing may make a traitor in Venice."

Vivaldi was upon the point of answering, when the Bravo moved towards the door. The noble did not attempt to stop him, for something about his presence seemed more like a vision of the past than a reality of the present; and while he yet gazed, the spot where Marco Martelino had stood was vacant, and in a moment more he heard the plash of his oars in the water.

CHAPTER IV.

The meeting of the conspirators—The doubts with regard to the Bravo—The plot—A sudden visit, and a strange servant for the Council of Ten.

WHEN Martelino left the house of Vivaldi, the storm had passed away, and the dark masses of clouds were slowly breaking apart and rolling off, while the bright moon once more rode majestically in a clear track. The Bravo pulled the boat to the spot from whence he had taken it, and then started back towards the city, keeping along by the most secluded ways, until he reached the palace of Marino Trivisano. Here he stopped, and after looking cautiously around, to assure himself that no one watched his movements, he approached the stairs which led down to the canal, and entered the house by the passage from the water. He was but a few moments in finding the private apartment of Trivisano, and when he did reach it, he found five Venetian nobles already collected there.

"Ah, here comes the very man!" remarked Trivisano, as the Bravo entered.

Martelino gazed around with a keen glance upon those who were assembled, and then said—

"Yes, I *am* the very man, and I trust I have come in season."

"Just in time," replied Trivisano, "for our friend Castello has but just arrived."

"Then let's to business at once," said the Bravo, "for I have other matters to attend to to-night."

"Other matters?" repeated Castello, in an interrogative tone.

"Yes."

The party exchanged significant glances, and appeared somewhat troubled, but Martelino quickly re-assured them by adding—

"I have got to set a watch upon that fellow Niccoli, the chief of the Ten; for he is on our track, and he must be removed."

"But he does not suspect any of us, does

FRANCIS VIVALDI AND THE BRAVO.

he ?" asked Trivisano, while a slight tremor shook his frame.

"Oh, no; he only suspects me, that's all," replied the Bravo. "You are all safe enough, at least for the present."

"If we are safe now," remarked one, by the name of Polani, "then why may we not remain safe ?"

"So you can, my masters," answered Martelino, "if you pursue the proper course; but you must be aware that there is but little safety, at all events, in the business in which we are engaged. Niccoli has his emissaries out in all directions, and you will be fortunate, if you escape him."

"Never fear for us, Martelino," said Trivisano; "but you must look well to yourself, for you are already suspected."

"Me suspected !" returned the Bravo, with a quick flash of his eagle eye, "I am known to be a conspirator. I have nothing to hide from the eyes of the Council's spies, unless, indeed, it be my connection with yourselves, and for your own sakes I shall keep that a secret. So, my masters, you need not be under any apprehensions from me, nor need you fear for yourselves on my account."

For some time after Martelino ceased speaking, no one seemed inclined to break the silence, but the nobles cast very furtive glances at each other, which appeared to indicate that some preliminary arrangements were expected before the main business was begun. At length these glances were all directed towards Trivisano, and feeling himself called upon to lead on, the old noble turned to Martelino and remarked—

"You will not think it strange, Marco, if we desire some pledge from you, before we trust you with more of our secrets. We do not even know who you are, nor from whence you came, nor have we the least assurance that you will not prove false and betray us, after all."

"And what assurance can I give you ?" asked the Bravo, without betraying the least difference on account of this questioning of his intentions. "If I can make you easy by any assurance of mine, I will do so; but as to who I am, and from whence I came, I am free to tell you that you will know no more than you do at present. You are upon the point of making arrangements for the overthrow of the Venetian government; you would dethrone the Doge, and place a king in his place. You would disrobe the councillors, and take their power into your own hands; and you think that the aspiring, proud-blooded nobles will assist you as soon as the ball is in motion, if you can but first

remove the dreaded Council of Ten. Marino Trivisano would be King of Venice! Ha, ha!—and what other secrets are there which you have among you ?"

Trivisano trembled, as Martelino so faithfully pictured their true designs; and the others felt no less uneasy; but Castello, who seemed more hardy than the others, even though his expectations were not so high, quickly answered—

"There are secrets, Bravo, which you do not know, and which cloak the most important points of our business. You may understand our ulterior designs, but you know not the means by which, the places where, nor the time when, we intend to carry them out; and these are the secrets which we have thought proper to withhold, until we receive some binding assurance that your lips nor actions shall ever betray us."

"Ha! ha! ha!" laughed Martelino, while a scornful expression dwelt upon his countenance; "you would keep these secrets, for fear I might betray you! Do you suppose, my lords, that the Council of Ten cares for such secrets? Suppose that arch spy, Niccoli, should know that the patricians, Trivisano, Dolfino, Polani, Masto, and Castello, had conceived the design which rests between you, what would he care for the means, the times, or the places? Ah, my masters! the breath of Marco Martelino even now holds the headsman's axe over your necks, and you had better beware how you trifle with his power. You have asked me to remove certain men from your path—men who must be removed before you can proceed with your designs. For certain sums of money I have agreed to do it, and I swear that it shall be done. All this work I must take upon my own shoulders, and Venice must never know that her own nobles are at the back of the dreaded Bravo; and yet you talk of my betraying you! If you fear, then you had better at once leave the path upon which you have entered; for I tell ye, conscript fathers, that stout hearts will be necessary ere you reach the goal. But, for your own ease, I will bind myself by any oath you choose to prescribe, only let it be done quickly, for I have told ye once that I have business elsewhere."

The conspirators evidently felt ill at ease beneath the quick, fiery glances of the Bravo, and Trivisano quickly answered—

"We want no oath, but you will not wonder that we ask you for a pledge of fidelity. We must trust you with our secrets, and we desire to feel that your interests are with us, for I assure you, that if we succeed you shall hold an important post under the already formed government."

"Then," replied Martelino, "I solemnly promise you that not one word, look, or action of mine shall tend to betray you, unless I first find that some of you have betrayed me. Will that suit you?"

All expressed themselves satisfied with this promise, for they at once saw that the interests of all concerned were so intimately connected, that one could not well betray the others without at the same time laying himself liable to the penalty of treason; and at a motion from Castello, Trivisano produced from his secret lockers a small roll of parchment.

"Here, my lords," said the old noble, as he unrolled the parchment, "is a complete list of all upon whom we may venture to operate. Of several of them I am sure, but the greater part will have to be approached with caution. To you, Castello, I give this list. You will at once recognize the names, as their owners all have seats in your department of the senate. To you, Dolfino, I give this list; those whose names are there enrolled are all in the eastern lobby. Polani and Masto, to you I give the list of those whose places are without the senate, and you must divide the duty as you see fit. For myself, I have reserved the nobles who are immediately about the person of the Doge. Now, I need not further impress you with the necessity of caution, for you must all be aware of the very dangerous ground upon which we stand."

Then turning to the Bravo, who had been a silent spectator of the apportionment of these duties, Trivisano continued—

"To you, Martelino, we give this list. There are only four names in it, but the men therein mentioned must be out of the way as soon as possible, for they are in the way most essentially, and until they are removed, we cannot with safety proceed."

The Bravo ran his eye over the four names upon the parchment, and then turning round upon those present, he said—

"Those shall be attended to; but are there not others who stand more in the way than do those whose names are here?"

"Not at present," replied Trivisano. "There are others who will come under your hand ere long, but their time has not yet come."

"And is this all with which you have to commission me to-night?"

"That is all," answered the noble, "and we shall not meet again till one week from to-night, when we expect that each will have a clear and safe account to render."

Thus commenced a plot which was calcu-lated by its projectors to entirely overthrow the Venetian government—or rather, we might say, it was the second or third time that the same plot had been started; for on one occasion, certainly, Trivisano had commenced the same, but circumstances had obliged him to relinquish its prosecution; but now the traitorous nobles commenced on a more safe and sure beginning, and already had their machinations assumed a fearful aspect for the peace and safety of the city. They had long known the daring and subtile character of Martelino, and in him they had found a man fit to cope with the dreaded Niccoli; for until chance threw the Bravo in their way, they had not dared to arouse the suspicions of the argus-eyed spy. In the Bravo, too, they thought they gained two objects: for, while he could be hired to do their murders, he would engross all the attention of Niccoli, thus leaving themselves to the furtherance of their plot. Of the fidelity of their agent they had not much doubt; but yet he was a man to be feared in more ways than one, and even though they had received his solemn promise, as the reader has already seen, still they dared not cross him, and after he had left the house, which he did as soon as he had received his instructions, the nobles held a long consultation upon the method in which he was to be treated.

"I tell you," said Castello, "Martelino is a fellow who may be trusted, if we only trust him. But if we betray the least signs of suspicion, you may be assured that we shall make his enmity, and to do that at the present time would be dangerous to us all."

"Castello is right," said Masto. "Did you not notice to-night how quickly his fire was aroused when we but hinted at the bare probability of his proving traitorous? We must place all confidence in the Bravo, or at least we must studiously endeavor to make him think that we do."

"But yet we must watch him narrowly," suggested Trivisano, "and that we can do without his noticing it, for he evidently feels but little sympathy with us further than gold is concerned."

It was past midnight when the nobles left the palace of Marino Trivisano, and pulling their short cloaks up over the lower part of their faces, they sought their own dwellings.

It might have been half an hour, perhaps more, after Trivisano's four associates left his dwelling, that the old noble sat by his table, busily engaged in writing. Whatever may have been the character of the matter which he was transferring from his plotting brain to the parchment, one thing is certain—it could not have been a work of honest intentions; for at the least noise from without he would start from his study, and instinctively lay his hand upon the written page before him. At length he leaned back from his work, seeming to study what next should be written, and while he yet gazed vacantly upon the characters already traced, he was startled by feeling a heavy hand upon his shoulder. Quick as thought, he dashed the parchment into his bosom, and leaped to his feet. Had the eyes of the old patrician rested upon the blood-stained executioner and his own death-warrant, he could not have been more terror-stricken than he was when they rested upon Niccoli, the *Spy of the Ten*. There was but one door to the apartment, and the key remained upon the inside of the lock, nor had it been turned.

"You seem somewhat startled, my lord," quietly remarked Niccoli, as something half way between a smile and a sneer curled upon his lip. "Perhaps you were not prepared for so unceremonious a visit."

"I was not certainly prepared for the intrusion of any one upon my private affairs, especially when my doors were locked," replied Trivisano, still trembling with doubt and fear as to the object of this strange visit.

"*Doors*, my lord Marino, are something which I seldom trouble, when my business is urgent," answered Niccoli, as he bent a peculiar look upon the old man.

For the first time a fearful thought flashed across the patrician's mind. He knew that the spy must have entered by some secret passage unknown to himself, and perhaps the whole conversation between the conspirators had been overheard by him. This thought for a moment almost took away his power of utterance, and settling back into his seat, he gazed vacantly upon his unwelcome visitor.

The plan of espionage by which nearly all the patrician dwellings contained secret passages, known only to the council and their spies, was not then near so general as it has been in later years; but the time has been when not a noble nor an officer of the government knew by what means the emissaries of the Ten could enter and leave their dwellings at pleasure. Even a patrician's own bed-chamber might be visited at any hour, and not a soul in the house be the wiser, while locks and keys were of no more account than would have been so many blades of grass. The doge himself knew not half the labyrinths of the ducal palace, and even what might appear to be the reserved right of royalty was set at naught by the keen-scented spies of the council. The lord Trivi-

sano knew that Niccoli possessed some strange secrets, and it is no wonder that the fear he thus exhibited should seize upon him; but it was quickly dispelled by the remark of the spy, for as soon as he noticed the agitation of his companion, he said—

"You seem ill, my lord, and I assure you I should not have intruded upon your privacy had not I been sent by the council?"

"And have the council been in session?" quickly asked Trivisano.

"Yes. I left but half an hour since."

The patrician's fears vanished in a moment; and so sudden was the change in the balance, that his feelings were as much elated as they had been before depressed, and with considerable vivacity he asked—

"And have they business with me?"

"They had business, but they have deputed it to me. By to-morrow's dawn I must be on my way to Padua, and it is necessary that you should have your instructions from me, or else I should have chosen another time to visit you. Now listen:—There is evidently a plot on foot in Venice against the government; how far it has gone, or how many are concerned in it, is more than we can ascertain. Now, you are looked upon by the council as one of the most experienced men in the senate, as well as one of the most loyal, and to you they desire to entrust a commission authorizing you, for the present, to exercise an espionage over such persons as you think proper. The only man against whom we have any grounds for suspicion is Marco Martelino; but he is evidently only a tool in the hands of others; and a most dangerous one he is, too, for he makes no secret of his intention to produce a radical change in the government, and yet we cannot get hold of him. He asserts that he is alone in the work; but we have reason to fear that some of the nobles are setting him on; and to you, my lord Marino, the council desire to give the charge of ascertaining the truth. Will you accept the duty?"

"With pleasure," quickly answered Trivisano.

There was more show of readiness in the answer than the noble had intended; but the duty was one so peculiarly adapted to aid him towards the consummation of his own ends, that he could not avoid manifesting a slight degree of the satisfaction which he felt, and as Niccoli seemed to take no notice of his manner, he thought it had not been noticed, so he quietly asked—

"When shall I commence?"

"On the morrow."

"And can you give me no names of those whom you have reason to suspect?"

"No," answered the spy, with a slight smile. "If we suspected any, we should want no assistance in condemning them. It is from the very lack of suspicion that we need your assistance."

"And suppose I should suspect some one?"

"Then watch till your suspicions are well grounded, and then report to the council."

"That I will do," returned the noble, "but I may after all turn out a poor hand at the trade."

"Never mind, my lord; you can do your best, at least. For all that Martelino has pretended to be alone in his plotting, still he has thrown out a hint that there be those in the senate who are to be feared. It is in that quarter that we would have you keep your eyes open."

Trivisano would have asked where and to whom the Bravo had done this, but before he could frame the question so as not to betray too much anxiety, the spy had turned the key in the door, and in a moment more he took his leave.

A curious servant had Niccoli secured in the person of Marino Trivisano! At least, so thought the old patrician himself.

CHAPTER V.

The return of reason—The fair visitor—Childhood's dreams—The discovery and its results—The interruption.

ON the sixth morning after the almost fatal disaster upon the canal, Alberte Lioni opened his eyes, with the light of reason to guide his vision, for the first time since he had been conveyed into the palace of the lord Vivaldi. The fever had been comparatively quick, for its seeds had been germinating in his system during a long period previous to the occurrence of the storm and exposure which had brought it to a crisis; but now that the delirium had passed, the most malignant features of the disease also disappeared—but still he felt weak and exhausted. As he tried to struggle through the cloud that hung over his memory, he found a blank there, which presented nothing but the kaleidoscopic remnants of a bright dream. Beyond that he could clearly remember the fearful storm, and the struggles he had undergone; then came the image of the sinking maiden, and his own efforts to save her. He remembered having seized the floating drapery, and he thought he had drawn her from the lashing waves; but here all became dim and indistinct. He had not seen her features; but something told him that they were young and beautiful, and an agonizing fear ran through his soul as the thought flashed across his mind that he might not have saved her.

As Alberte's mind began to gather strength, he gazed around the apartment to see if he was in his own chamber; but he was not so much astonished at finding himself in a strange place, as he was by the luxury and magnificence of all about him. How much he might have wondered at the strangeness of his situation, it is impossible to tell, for hardly had he satisfied himself that he was not still dreaming, when the door cautiously opened, and the lord Vivaldi entered. The old man saw at a glance the favorable change which had taken place, and approaching the bed-side, he said:

"You are better, my young friend?"

"I am weak and faint," replied Alberte; "but I think I must have been much worse."

"Indeed you have. For two or three days the physician had serious doubts with regard to your recovery."

"For two or three days!" repeated the youth, in surprise. "And have I been sick so long?"

"This is the sixth day since you were brought hither," replied Vivaldi; "but you are now out of danger, and by care you may soon be well."

For several moments Alberte pressed his hand upon his brow, and at length he raised his eyes, and asked—

"Can you tell me if the girls are safe whom I would have rescued from the storm?"

"They are, my noble youth, and a father's gratitude shall ever be yours."

"And were they your daughters?"

"One of them was," replied the old noble. "She is my only child, and you have preserved to me a jewel worth more than life itself. But now that you are in your sound mind, I would ask you your name; for since you have been here, you have avoided the question with a determination which no persuasion could shake; and though on all other subjects you have been rambling and unguarded, still upon the subject of your family you have maintained the utmost reserve."

"My name," answered Alberte, while a troubled hesitancy marked his manner, "is Alberte Lioni."

"Does your family reside in Venice?"

The youth gazed for a moment into the face of his interlocutor, and then his eyes filled with tears. He was not weak-minded, nor was he covetous of sympathy; but sickness had unstrung his nerves, and as his mind ran back to the fate of his family name, he could not restrain the overflowing of a heart that held a large space for the sacred memory of a father. The old noble saw that the sick youth was too ill to bear such excitement as his question had occasioned, and he kindly said,

"I did not mean to pry into your secrets, my young friend, nor would I utter a syllable that could pain you. Your physician will be here, ere long, and until then you had better remain quiet; so, for the present, I will leave you to repose."

"Stay one moment," urged Alberte, as the noble was upon the point of turning away: "May I not know under whose roof I now am?"

"You are in the palace of the patrician Vivaldi."

"Francis Vivaldi?"

"Yes."

"And are you he?"

"Yes."

"Was it Isidora Vivaldi whom I saved from a watery grave?" asked Alberte, as he vainly endeavored to raise himself upon his elbow.

"It was," replied Vivaldi, much surprised at the strange agitation of the young man. "Were you ever acquainted with her?"

The old man bent a scrutinising gaze upon Alberte as he asked the question, but he received no direct answer. The youth only murmured to himself—

"Then 'twas a dream of boyhood that has been haunting me. Oh, that I could—"

He did not finish the sentence, for he caught the inquiring gaze of Vivaldi fixed so earnestly upon him, that he immediately stopped his wandering thoughts, and returning the look of his host, he added—

"You may be surprised, sir, at my strange behaviour, but you may yet have it all explained; and, in the meantime accept my assurance, that in me your roof covers one who never did aught to tarnish the honor of his manhood."

"I believe you," quickly answered the old noble—and once more urging upon his charge the necessity of remaining as quiet as possible, he left the apartment.

When the physician came, he made no hesitation in pronouncing his patient out of danger, and after giving directions for the administering of some slight restorative, he left, with the assurance that Alberte would need nothing but rest and quiet to reinstate him to his former health.

On the second morning after the call of the doctor, Alberte was able to sit up in his chair, and in about an hour after he had donned his dressing-gown, and while he was busily engaged in poring over an old manuscript, which lay upon the table at his side, he was aroused by the sound of a light foot-fall in the upper hall, and shortly after he heard a light rap at his door. He bade whoever might be there to enter, and the next moment his eyes rested upon the form of her who had been the object of his delirium-caused visions. The heart of Alberte Lioni leaped wildly in his bosom as the bright form approached him, and with a strong effort he tried to rise to his feet, but a tiny hand held him down.

"Not too fast," said the new comer, in a voice so sweet and soft, that it sounded to the invalid like the breathings of an angel; "I fear you are yet too weak to extend much courtesy to visitors."

A kind smile rested upon her lips as she spoke, and beneath its encouraging influence the tongue of Alberte found its power, for he extended his hand, and uttered—

"I am sure I cannot be mistaken—you are she whom I saw sinking beneath the waters of the canal."

"And she whom you saved from a terrible death," added the girl, as she looked with a peculiar gratitude into the face of her preserver.

"Then you are the daughter of the lord Vivaldi?"

"Yes—his only child," returned she; and then gazing for a moment upon the pale countenance of Alberte, she added—

"And my father tells me that your name is Alberte Lioni?"

There was a peculiarity in the expression of Isidora, as she uttered this, that savored somewhat of an interrogation, and its manner called up a strange feeling in the young man's bosom. The fair girl noticed the appearance of her companion, and perhaps attributing it to a natural reserve, she continued in a frank and open manner:

"Perhaps I feel more acquainted than you do, for this is the first time that you have seen me to recognize me, while I have been a constant visitor at your bedside since your sickness."

"Pardon me, lady," quickly replied Alberte, "if I have appeared disconcerted—but your image calls up such pleasant dreams that I cannot force my mind from the bright fields of the past."

"That is perhaps the result of your fevered imagination during your sickness. The more pointed circumstances of your delirium, I suppose, appear like dreams to you now."

Whether Isidora said this for the sake of hiding some deep feeling that had been called into existence by the remark of her companion, or whether she said it for the purpose of conversation, we cannot say; but one thing is certain, the manner of its delivery plainly indicated that her thoughts were not with her words. This conclusion seemed also to come to the mind of Alberte; but he appeared to take little notice of it, for he was too deeply buried in his own reflections; and raising his large lustrous eyes to the face of the girl before him, he replied—

"No, lady, the dreams of which I speak date further back than that. Your image is indeed connected with the visions of my late wandering, but 'tis the bright page of happier days upon which my minds rests; but alas! for me all that remains is the privilege of treasuring up the memories of joys which can never be mine again. I can dwell upon the bright hopes of the past, but the future contains no happy chance for their fulfilment."

Isidora Vivaldi felt a strange flutter at her heart as those large bright eyes rested upon her, and her own mind seemed struggling to drink in some vision wherein she had seen them before; but memory refused to reveal the secret, and with a sensation of strange doubts, she asked—

"Did you ever know me before that dreadful night on which I came so near my death?"

"I did not know you then, fair lady, for if I had, these hands would never have refused their office till you had been safe."

"Nor did they," quickly replied Isidora, "for the man who took us to the landing-stairs says you had safely secured us from harm."

"Well," answered Alberte, "let that be as it may, I did the duty alone which every man owes to his fellows, and I am happy to know that my efforts were blessed with success. But I did not answer your question. I *did* know a bright-eyed, laughing girl when I was a boy, and I called her Isidora."

"And she called you—"

"Her *father* learned her to call me her *little husband.*"

Isidora Vivaldi gazed intently into the face of her companion, but there was no trembling in her manner. Her heart, even, almost ceased to beat, as the misty veil fluttered for a moment in the air of doubt and then slowly arose from the picture she had struggled to call up. She laid her hand upon the shoulder of Alberte, and said—

"Your name was Marcello!"

"You have spoken rightly," replied Alberte, as he gazed earnestly into the face of his fair companion, to see what effect the revelation might have upon her.

The young man had spoken differently from what he would have done under other circumstances, but his sickness had spread a kind of childish confidence over his disposition, and he realized not that his plain and summary rehearsal of the past was out of character, under the present situation of the lady and himself; but, be that as it may, his bosom swelled with a peculiar and strange emotion, as he found that the eyes of the gentle Isidora were beaming with the sunlight of a love which could not be hidden by her artless nature, and he almost felt in reality that the days of childhood were once more brimming in his cup of life. Already had he framed his mind to a realization of those joys once more, when the door of the apartment opened, and the lord Vivaldi entered.

Isidora cast one look upon Alberte Lioni, but with all his powers of mind he could not analyze it. There was much of affection in it, but there was also so much of some other feeling, that he remained in a doubt as dark as the cloud which he had sought to remove —and before he could seek for an explanation in another glance of those bright eyes, she had left the room.

CHAPTER VI.

The father's misgivings, and the extracted promise —The old man's avowal—Alberte's resolution— Hopes and doubts.

OR some time after Isidora left the room, the old noble gazed in silence upon the young invalid. There was in his gaze a strange mixture of admiration and something very nearly akin to misgiving, and a slight tremulousness marked his voice, as he said—

"My young friend, I have seen enough of the world to understand that straightforward frankness is always the best principle of action, more especially when we have honorable men to deal with, and as I look upon you as one of that class, I shall expect that there will be no reserve in our conversation at this time."

"I never yet deceived any one," replied Alberte, while his pale cheek was flushed with an unwonted glow, "and I trust I shall not be suspected of doing it now."

"I did not suspect it," answered Vivaldi, "but I merely mentioned the subject, because the matter I am about to broach is a recalling of old affairs, and perhaps you might think that a silent reserve would be justifiable."

"My lord Vivaldi," said the youth, as he bent his attention towards the countenance of his host, "whatever you have to say may be said at once, and I know of nothing in the past or present that I should blush to own. I do not hesitate to tell you, however, that there are circumstances which I would not make a subject of general remark; but to you, sir, I know not that I shall feel in the least reserved upon any of them."

"Then," returned the old patrician, "I would first ask, are you not the son of Giovanni Marcello?"

"Such was my father's name," answered Alberte, without hesitation.

"The old senator who was banished for treason?"

"So reads the record upon the archives of the Council of Ten," replied the young man, while the nervous twitching of the muscles about the lips and the corners of the mouth betrayed an intense feeling; "but God knows that the Ten judged him wrongfully, and when my poor father died, Venice lost one of her firmest friends."

"What you say may be true," replied Vivaldi, "and I may even assure you that I have ever had doubts with regard to the lord Marcello's guilt; but you must be aware that by the action of the council, the name of your family is stricken from the patrician list in the senate."

"You are perfectly right, sir," returned Alberte, with a tone of deep irony. "The council took away all they could—the mere bauble of a name; but the true nobility of nature—that principle which elevates man above his fellows—is an emanation from the soul of Deity, and all the councils in the world cannot take it from the man who is so fortunate as to possess it. I would not ask for a rank in Venice which is held by a tenure so light, that the falsehoods of plotting men could wrest it from me. My father looks down upon the city for which he would have readily given up his life, and sees with indifference the paltry baubles for which men

shed each other's blood; he has his home now in that fair land where neither the ducal bonnet nor the regal diadem can cover a mote of sin, and I trust that his memory may not be connected with aught that is unpleasant for the mind of his son to dwell upon."

"Fear not that I shall do that," replied Vivaldi, who could not but admire the noble and independent spirit of the youth. "When you were first brought to my dwelling, I thought I recognized in your countenance the likeness of some one with whom I had been acquainted, but I could not arrive at any definite conclusion, and your name tended still more to blind me; but as soon as you had recovered, I at once hit upon the truth —I knew that you were the son of my unfortunate friend, and I immediately came to the determination to speak to you upon a subject which has much interest for all concerned. You probably remember some of the peculiar relations which existed between our families before the death of your father?"

"Some of them," returned Alberte, while a slight shade of melancholy passed over his countenance, "I can never forget; but they are only as the landmarks of the past, from which I date a new existence—an existence which must take its weal or woe from the moral tone it bears. I know too well, that henceforth I have no rank or station upon which to found my hopes. I am aware, my lord Vivaldi, of what you would say, and I know, too, that the subject is one of a delicate nature, but I assure you that you need not fear. Now that I have naught but the true manhood of an honest and upright soul for my portion, I know that I may not aspire to those favors which are reserved for the lot of the patrician."

Vivaldi felt ill at ease beneath the cutting words of his young companion. There was no sarcasm, nor was there much of irony in them; but still he felt their force from their truthfulness, and he knew, too, that he was forced to acknowledge the "nobility" of men who had not half the merit that was possessed by young Lioni. Years before, when Giovanni Marcello held a seat in the senate, by the side of himself, Francis Vivaldi had looked upon him as his truest and noblest friend, and in their social capacity the two nobles were also firm and tried friends. While the son of the one and the daughter of the other were still children, they had been affianced by their fond fathers, and the youthful Alberte had loved the gentle being who was thus destined for him with a love as deep as could have been felt by the more experienced in years. The fair Isidora, too, had given the

ALBERTE AND ISIDORA.

whole of her young heart where her father had so confidently given her hand, and ere her eighth summer had shed its flowers about her path, she had learned to look upon her childish playmate as her future husband. Thus stood matters between the families of Marcello and Vivaldi, when the former was accused of participating in a plot for the subversion of the government, and, by the direct evidence of several of the nobles, condemned to banishment.

Had Vivaldi, when his former friend was first driven from his native city, let all matters drop among things that were past and gone, which related to their previous connection, all might have been well; but instead of pursuing such a course, he sought, by argument and entreaty, to induce his daughter to forget young Marcello, seeming not to remember that such was the way to fix his image more vividly in her young mind. Years rolled on, and still the heart of Isidora was with him who in childhood's hours had won her soul's best and purest love. The more her father tried to urge her, the more closely twined the love he would have eradicated, and more than once had he experienced the mortification of seeing her refuse the hands of some of the noblest lords of Venice.

When Alberte first returned to his native city, after his father had obtained permission for him to return to his studies, he had most studiously avoided all those friends with whom, in times past, they had been intimate; and as his family name had been taken from him, hardly any of the nobles knew him. They knew, of course, that he had permission from the council to return, but they knew not his person. The living love of Isidora Vivaldi, however, had seen through the veil; and when she first beheld the delirium-wrought countenance of her preserver, though she did not recognize the playmate of her childhood, still her heart sent forth an instinctive feeling of affection, which, had she sought to explain, would have baffled all her power; and when she first learned from the lips of the youth the truth, she only heard what her soul had already felt.

The lord Vivaldi, from the moment he had seen Alberte after the return of his reason, had recognized the son of Marcello, and the father's heart soon became alarmed for the safety of his daughter. He knew that Isidora still cherished the memory of her early love, and he had determined to seek the present interview for the purpose of guarding against the evil he so much feared, but even now he almost wished that the laws of Venice did not forbid the marriage of patricians with the lower ranks; for there was so much to love and respect in the character of the youth, that his heart not only felt for him, but his judgment told him that nowhere could his daughter find a better husband. But the laws of the patrician rank were imperative, and he had no alternative, so he said, as the youth closed his last remark—

"You may have occasion to speak bitterly of those circumstances which have so affected you, but still you cannot blame me for the course I am obliged to pursue. I have not supposed that you would take the least advantage of the obligations we are under to you to do aught that could do me harm; but I know the human heart too well not to be aware that there are circumstances over which the judgment holds no control, and among them is that of love. You know that the time was when you were led to look upon my daughter as your promised bride, and I knew not but that your heart might still bear the same feeling towards her. If such was the case, I feared that, by leaving you both to follow your own inclinations, you might be led to a state where much unhappiness would be the only result, for you well know that I must bow to the laws of the land, however much my own feelings might dictate to the contrary. You may think that I have spoken needlessly upon this subject, and perhaps I have—but a word in season can do no harm."

"I appreciate your motives," said Alberte, "nor do I take the least offence; but I will not hide from you the fact that I have ever loved your daughter with the whole fervor of my soul, nor can my heart ever be given to another; but so long as I remain a guest beneath your roof, I will not broach to her the subject."

"I thank you, my young friend, for your frankness, and I assure you that a heavy load is removed from my bosom; for your position is one so peculiar, that I feared you might turn a deaf ear to my entreaties."

"Methinks, sir," replied Alberte, "that you should give yourself little uneasiness on your daughter's account, for she would not surely bestow her love upon a poor, trampled youth."

"She may never have ceased to feel—"

Vivaldi did not close the sentence; for as he caught the expression of his young companion's countenance, he was startled by the unwonted fire that burned in his large, dark eyes, and he at once saw that he might have said too much; but he had no time for reflection, for Alberte quickly said—

"Tell me, sir—tell me truly—I swear by the memory of my sainted father, that I will never take advantage of your answer—does your daughter still love me?"

There was a peculiar wildness in the youth's manner, and as he closed he grasped the old man by the shoulder, and waited anxiously for an answer.

Vivaldi knew not how to reply. He knew that if he told the truth, he should tell the youth that Isidora loved him most fervently —that for years she almost lived upon the memory of her early affection; but he feared to tell this—he feared to inspire the heart of young Lioni with so baseless a hope.

"You said, my lord Vivaldi," urged Alberte, as he noticed the old man's hesitancy, "that you hoped we should both be frank and straight-forward, and I trust that you will be so now. Your own manner convinces me that Isidora has not forgotten me; and if you will tell me the whole truth, I shall have no questions to ask the lady, you may rest assured of that."

"Well," returned the old noble, while his voice trembled with an ill-defined fear, "I will tell you the truth. My daughter loves you too well for her own happiness, and for this reason have I sought this interview. From the moment when your father was first banished from Venice, she has blindly cherished the love with which I once permitted her to become possessed, and even now I fear that she has recognized in you the object of her early love—and if such is the case, the circumstances of your having saved her life will by no means be calculated to quench the flame."

"She has recognized me, sir," replied Alberte, as he sank back into his chair, and placed his hands over his face. For a few moments he sat thus, and at length, as he brushed away a tear that started to his eye, he rose from his chair, supported by a sudden and strange strength, and laying his hand upon the old man's shoulder, he continued, almost in a whisper, but with a most intense earnestness—

"Once more, sir, I ask your answer. Tell me—not hastily, but calmly and considerately —were I once more restored to the estate in which I was born—were I but clothed in the nobility which my patrician father lost— were I but permitted by the council and senate once more to wear the name of Marcello—might I have your permission to wed the lady Isidora?"

"Be calm, I pray you," urged Vivaldi, as he forced the youth back to his chair. "Your excitement will certainly bring you back to your bed again."

"Tell me, sir," still persisted Alberte, "if you would quell the fire of a heart which is racked almost to bursting—if, under the circumstances I have pictured, you would grant that I might win and wear the jewel you so much prize."

"Certainly, my young friend," replied the old noble, as his countenance underwent a variety of changes; "if you could honestly obtain the rank of which you speak, I should have no objection to your suit, for I have already assured you that I have the most implicit confidence in your honor as a man; and only the laws, over which I have no control, force me to the position I have taken. But the picture you have drawn, I fear, can never be realized, for the council seldom reconsider their actions."

"But I know that my father was innocent; and suppose I could prove it to the full satisfaction of the council, would they not then reverse their decision with regard to his estates?"

"Of course they would."

"And may not a just God place in my hands the means of proving this—so important a truth?"

"You can certainly try," replied Vivaldi, in a desponding tone; "but I much fear that you will never succeed. The lord Marcello had a fair and impartial trial, and—"

"Fair and impartial, did you say?" interrupted Alberte. "And can the trial which results in the open disgrace and ruin of one of the noblest men of Venice, even though he be innocent of even a thought against his government, be fair and impartial?"

"The evidence, my young friend, was too strong for a doubt, and hence the decision of the council was in accordance with it. I can see nothing which makes the action in the case at all unfair."

"Tell me, my lord," said young Lioni, while his eye beamed with the fire of a conscious right, "do you believe the evidence that was given against my father? Do you not know that much of that evidence was false—basely false?"

"You ask me now," returned Vivaldi, who was evidently much embarrassed by the close corner in which he was placed, "to impeach some of the nobles in Venice."

"But how can an expression of your opinion be an impeachment?"

"You are probably aware that I am one of the state inquisitors, and that my authority, combined with that of my two associates, is superior to even the Doge himself, and hence such an accusation on my part would be a certain impeachment."

"But I assure you, sir, that whatever answer you may make, it shall never go from my lips; but I would fain know whether there be not some among my father's old friends who believe him innocent of the crime for which he suffered."

"Well," at length answered Vivaldi, "I do believe that Giovanni Marcello was innocent of any crime, although at the time he was condemned I believed most of the evidence against him. You were too young to understand anything that occurred; but in your father's private cabinet, within a drawer—to the lock of which only himself possessed a key—was found a written plan of the whole plot; but at the present time I have reason to believe that he knew not how it came there."

"I thank you, sir, most sincerely, for this avowal of your belief; and if there be others who believe the same, I may yet make out the evidence I need, and may God enable me to do it!"

"Amen!" fervently uttered Vivaldi; and then gazing for a moment into the working countenance of the youth, he continued—

"I must leave you now, for business calls me; but I trust you will bear in mind what I have said."

"Fear not, sir," answered Alberte. "You may trust to my honor."

After warmly returning the affectionate grasp of his young friend, the lord Vivaldi left the room.

Ah, Alberte Lioni, where now are all thy dreams of nature's nobility? Where now is thy goal of an honorable happiness in the lower walks of life? One single glance from the eyes of your childhood's queen, and the assurance that she loves you still, have set your heart upon the bauble of lordly rank. On, then! and learn to know how troublous is the path you have chosen. The love of the fair Isidora has lifted the clouds for the moment, but be assured that they will settle again, darker and more fearful than ever!

CHAPTER VII.

The second meeting of the conspirators—The Council of Ten, and their peculiar traits—The plot thickens.

THE week which was to intervene before the second meeting of the conspirators slipped slowly by, and the appointed time found the five leading nobles already at the palazzo of Trivisano, nor had they to wait long before Martelino also made his appearance. The Bravo came in with a firm step, and the dark business in which they were engaged seemed to have no terrors for him; for while the others cast trembling, furtive glances about them at every breath which swept through the lattice, he was cool and self-possessed. Marco Martelino, terrible as was his name, with a heavy price set upon his head, and proscribed throughout the commonwealth, knew not what it was to fear.

"Well, my masters," exclaimed he, as he doffed the heavy slouched hat, "how goes the plot?"

"Right well," returned Trivisano, rubbing his hands in high glee. "More of the nobles are open to rebellion than we had anticipated."

A dark cloud passed over the Bravo as he heard this, and quickly facing the conspiring patricians, he said,—

"And have ye so soon bruited your plans abroad? How know ye, Trivisano, that many of the nobles are open for rebellion!"

"How now, thou—"

"Hold, Castello," exclaimed Masto, as the former was framing an angry retort to the Bravo.

"And for what shall I hold?" returned the hot-headed Castello. "Shall we be browbeaten by yon swarthy Bravo?"

"Methinks, my good lords and masters," said Martelino, while his towering form added a strange power to the command of his flashing eyes, "that ye had better all hold. But a week has yet passed, and still you have stirred extensively among the senators. Do you think that the nobles of Venice are all fools, that you can toy with them as you would with children? To how many, Trivisano, have you yet spoken?"

"There be fifteen who have been sounded."

"And you are sure of how many?"

"Well," returned the old noble, slightly trembling beneath the steady gaze of the Bravo, "we are not sure of any yet."

"So, my lords, you have given your deeplaid plans to the fickle winds of suspicion at least, and yet you have not gained a *soldi*. I tell you, once more, that the eyes of the spy are open, and ye know not who may be his emissaries. Perhaps some of those very men whom you number upon your list are among his tools."

"Ha, ha, ha, Martelino," laughed Trivisano, "you are out there; for Niccoli has given to me the whole charge of sifting out this matter."

Here the old noble explained to the Bravo the particulars of his interview with the spy of the Ten, and showed how, under such a commission, he had been able to broach the subject without fear of detection; for behind the cloak of his duty he could easily hide his ulterior designs.

"That may alter the case some," replied Martelino; "but still you must remember that I have the most to bear, and you owe it to me that no danger comes from any misadventure of yours."

"Never fear for that," returned Trivisano. "I have been cautious, and I find that many of the nobles like not the Council of Ten. It has too much power over their liberties."

"What portion of their liberties?" quietly asked the Bravo, as he bent a meaning look upon the old man. "The nobles of Venice have certainly the widest range of any in the world, and there lies the trouble. The Council of Ten even looks with a kind of approbation upon all the sins against morality of which the Venetian noble is guilty. No, my lords, the council is guilty in the very liberty it grants to those of your own rank, and hence I war against its evils. Your patrician may be black as night with the stains of debauchery and moral degradation, and still no notice is taken of the sin; and such fools are the pleasure-seeking nobles, that they see not that the council is answering its own ends in their very course of reckless libertinism."

"You speak in riddles, Marco," said Castello, who was struck with the peculiarity of these ideas. "Pray, tell us, how can these small sins of the nobility answer any ends of the council?"

"I will tell you," answered the Bravo. "You know that the Council of Ten, with the three state inquisitors, are superior to all other powers in Venice. Even the Doge himself knows not what they do, nor what may be their intentions, and also the senate has no business with their private transactions. The nobility of Venice are all under their fearful power; and the slightest breath of treason may take the patrician from the palace, or the Doge from his ducal chair, and he never may know, even upon the scaffold, who have been his accusers. Now, such a power must necessarily depend upon the people for its existence; and do you not see that in proportion as the nobility lose their popularity with the people, in the same proportion does that council which protects the state from civil discord, gain strength; for the people have nothing to fear from the Council of Ten, while their rulers have everything? Thus, while a virtuous, humane, and charitable nobility would be loved and respected by the masses, on the contrary, the dissolute, debauched, and intemperate will find no sympathy with them; and while the former would find protection from any hasty conviction, the latter would look in vain for aid. But, my masters, though this in the abstract might work well for the state, still it has its evils, and great ones, too; for so confident have the council become in their power, that even the innocent man may suffer; and should his accusers refuse to appear, he may be beheaded without having the privilege of facing them."

All saw the truth of Martelino's statement; and for several moments afterwards a dead silence prevailed, which was at length broken by Trivisano, who said—

"There is much truth in what you say, and it behoves us that we come not within the clutches of the council, for we might rest assured of but little sympathy. But now, what have you done towards the consummation of our plans?"

"As yet, but little," replied the Bravo. "I have studied the best modes of operation, and ere long I shall commence."

"But Francis Vivaldi must be the first removed," said Trivisano, while a slight shudder passed through his frame as he pronounced the name of that powerful nobleman.

"And so he shall be," returned Martelino, "as soon as the proper time comes. He may live for two weeks yet, but he shall be out of the way before his presence can do you any harm."

"Ah, another brat has turned up who may yet stand in our path," said Castello. Perhaps he would have said more, but at that moment his eye caught the troubled look of Trivisano, and he hesitated.

"Another?" asked the Bravo, as a frown gathered upon his brow. "And who is it?"

"Oh, nothing—no one," returned the lord Marino, while an agitation which he could not suppress crept over him. "Castello merely alluded to a circumstance which I mentioned to him this morning, but I have found myself entirely mistaken. The person to whom I alluded is not what I at first suspected."

Martelino may have looked as though he was satisfied with this explanation, but when, some half hour later, he left the place, there was a bitter curl upon his lips; and could the conspirators have read his heart, they would have known he was far from being satisfied.

"You did wrong, Castello, in so carelessly making mention of that subject before the Bravo," said Trivisano, as soon as he was sure that Martelino was out of hearing.

"But I thought that he was to do the work?"

"Why, no. The youth must be removed without the knowledge of the Bravo, for his case is so connected with the old plot, that we should have to explain to Martelino the whole of our former conspiracy, and then we should be wholly in his power. If the boy would but keep quiet he might live, but the position he has now taken will be dangerous, for the lord Marcello was a great favorite with the people, so much so, that the council did not dare to behead him, even though the first sentence was to that effect; and should his son now make a stir to prove his father's innocence, he would find friends on every hand, and if I am not much mistaken, old Vivaldi will aid him in the prosecution of his design."

"But how do you know that old Marcello's son is really engaged in such a work?" asked Masto.

"Because he has said so, and Vivaldi so informed the person who told me of it; and should he succeed in his designs, it might bring the whole of us into immediate condemnation. The youth has passed under the name of Lioni, and but a short time since he saved the life of Vivaldi's daughter, in consequence of which he will most assuredly receive the old man's aid."

"And is the youth still at the chief's house?"

"Yes," returned Trivisano; "but he walked out to-day, and I doubt not that ere long he will be able to pull his gondola upon the canal."

"How do you intend to finish him?" asked Castello, as he began to realize the trouble that might ensue.

"I have the means at hand," returned Trivisano, "and while the Bravo finishes Vivaldi, leave the boy to me."

When the conspirators separated that night, a strong net was woven around the fate of Alberte Lioni. The hungry vulture was hovering over his path!

CHAPTER VIII.

The invalid once more upon the canal—The young stranger—An unexpected offer—The vulture has settled upon his prey.

STRENGTH had once more returned to our youthful hero, and he waited only for the full enjoyment of his health before he entered, heart and soul, upon the work he had laid out. Isidora had learned the whole truth, and her heart beat with a vivid hope as she looked forward to the time when Alberte should claim her hand. Hers was a heart that could hold no deceit, and she frankly avowed the love she held for her young preserver, while with all her assurances of fidelity, she urged him on in the path he marked out. She knew that there were lords in Venice who sought her hand, and she furthermore knew that to one of them her father had given hopes of obtaining her. This was Carolus Trivisano, the only son of the noble with whom the reader is already acquainted. Twice had she peremptorily refused his suit, but still he sought by all possible means to win some mark of her esteem, nor could any coldness on her part drive him from her. At their last meeting, young Trivisano had expressed himself in a manner ill calculated to beget any very agreeable feelings in the bosom of the young lady, and he had even thrown out some dark hints, which, had he sufficient power, might have created alarm in Isidora's bosom. But, however beautiful and honorable might have been the aspirants to the hand of Isidora Vivaldi, she could never have given them her love, for her heart dwelt wholly in the atmosphere of the past, and from the recollections of childhood she brought the ideal of her affection. Now that ideal had become real. In Alberte she found the talismanic mirror from which her own love was reflected, and here her heart fluttered for a moment, like the troubled needle as it seeks its true point in the north, and then settles gently down to rest in its home.

The sun had passed the meridian, and was gently sinking in its western track, when Alberte Lioni stepped down from the palazzo of the lord Vivaldi, and entered a small gondola which lay moored at the foot of the steps. Having cast off the line which held the boat's head, he dipped the light oars into the water and started off down the canal. Once more the young man's heart bounded with happy impulse as he found himself careering over the sparkling water, and his nostrils opened to the fresh air as it came sweeping up from the Adriatic, as though they would have drunk in the freshness which had been so long denied them. The change from a sick chamber to the open canal was so agreeable to the youth's senses, that he hardly realized the fact, that even in the latter place it was necessary to use circumspection, for in his blindness of ecstatic pleasure he had come very near upsetting several of his more staid and circumspect neighbors; and it was not until he ran directly upon a gondola, which was crossing ahead of him, that he began to realize the necessity of keeping in mind the fact, that there were others upon the canal besides himself. As he shot clear of the gondola, against which he had so unceremoniously run, he turned to ask the pardon of whoever might be in it, but before he could do so, it had been pulled out of hearing. He saw, however, that it contained only an old gentleman and a youth about his own age; and thinking that no harm had been done, he set his oars once more in motion, determined to be more careful for the rest of the ride.

Alberte Lioni did not notice the manœuvre of the gondola which had attempted to cross his track, nor did he notice that the collision had been the result of design on the part of the stranger, and more than all the rest, he did not know that that old gentleman was the lord Trivisano; but such was the fact.

Alberte rowed on till his relaxing muscles began to indicate that he had gone as far as prudence would allow, when he turned the head of his boat towards home. He had not rowed more than half the distance back, when he saw a gondola approaching him from the opposite side of the canal, and as he slightly backed his oars so as to allow it to pass, its occupant, who was a young man, hailed him.

"Will you stop a moment?" asked the stranger, as he pulled up alongside.

"Certainly," replied Alberte, slightly wondering what could be wanted.

"Is your name Lioni?"

"It is."

"Alberte Lioni?"

"Yes."

"You once went by another name."

"How know you that?" quickly asked Alberte.

"Never mind how; it is enough for the present that I know it."

"Well—and what then?"

"You are the son of Giovanni Marcello, or at least you were when he was living."

"Since you know so much," replied Alberte, "you may as well go on boldly with what you have to say."

"I knew I was right," said the stranger, as he cast a small line over the row-lock of Alberte's boat, so that they might the more easily be kept together, and then lowering his voice, he continued—

"I have a secret for the ears of Marcello's son."

"A secret!" repeated Alberte, in surprise.

"Yes; and one which it might benefit him to know, would he accomplish a work which might place him once more in the station he has lost."

"Speak on, sir," uttered Alberte.

"Would you know the secret?"

"If it can benefit me, certainly."

"You think that your father was innocent of the crime for which he suffered."

"I know it."

"But can you prove it?"

"Not yet; but I trust the time is not far distant when I shall be able to do so."

"But suppose I could place in your power the means even now."

"You, sir?"

"Yes."

"Can you do it?"

"Yes."

"And will you do it?" exclaimed Alberte, as he started from his seat, and fixed an earnest gaze upon the stranger.

"If I had not intended so to do, I should certainly not have held out the hope," returned he. "And now, if you will but follow me a short distance, I will give you the necessary information."

"But why not do it here?"

"Here?" iterated the stranger. "That might be done if there were not papers which it is necessary you should possess."

"If they are far out of the way," suggested Alberte, "I might find my strength inadequate to the task of rowing back again; for I am but just relieved from a bed of sickness, and already my nerves begin to weaken from the exercise I have now taken."

"Oh, let not that trouble you," good-naturedly answered Alberte's companion, "for I will row you myself. You can make fast your boat to one of the rings here, and give it in charge to the stair-master, and I will return you hither in half an hour at the farthest."

"Then let it be so," returned our hero, as he sat back upon his seat, and turned the head of his gondola towards the landing-stairs.

Alberte's strange guide gave a few hurried

words of instruction to the man who was to take charge of the gondola, and then, as both were seated in his own boat, he remarked—

"We had better put on our masks. Have you one with you?"

"No," answered young Lioni, looking up in surprise. "That is something I do not carry with me. But what need have we of disguise?"

"Why, you must readily see that some one has much interest in keeping your father's innocence a secret; and although I would help you, still I am not willing to bring down the wrath of others upon my head in consequence, and to guard against the occurrence of such an evil, it would suit me much better were we both masked. I have one that will suit you, and with your permission I will lend it to you."

Alberte knew not that he had an enemy in the world, for he had never harbored an evil thought against any man, and in the purity of his intentions he had no heart to impute guile to others, so without hesitation he accepted the proffered mask, and placed it upon his face. But for all this he could not repress a feeling of apprehension; yet it was so vague and ill-defined that he thought little of it, imputing it rather to an excitement produced by the expectations that had been raised by his companion's offer than to anything else.

Instead of pulling his gondola up the main canal, the stranger turned into one of the narrow outlets, and after a circuitous route of about fifteen minutes, he hauled up at the foot of the marble steps which led to the palace of the patrician Trivisano.

"Do you stop here?" asked Alberte, as he at once recognized the home of his childhood.

"Yes," returned the other. "Make no remark, but follow me as quickly as possible, and noiselessly, too."

A strange feeling of misgiving crept over the soul of Alberte Lioni, as he found himself once more treading the marble pavement of his father's halls. He could not but fear that all was not right, for if there was a man living who would not that the secret of Marcello's innocence should be betrayed, that man was surely the lord Trivisano, and it seemed improbable that one whose interests were not connected with his, should thus, in broad daylight, enter his dwelling for the purpose of removing so important papers as those which had been promised. He had not much time for reflection, however, for his guide soon stepped into a small closet, and as he returned with a lighted lamp in his hand, he said—

"Be quiet now, and we shall soon have all that you need. Trivisano is out, and from one of the servants, whom I can trust, I have received the keys to his private vault. Follow on as fast as possible."

The objects which seemed familiar to our youthful hero began to grow less and less frequent, and he soon knew that he was in that department which lay below the canal, and which in boyhood he had never dared to explore.

"Hold!" exclaimed Alberte. "Until I have some assurance of what is to follow, I shall go no further. If you seek to do me the favor you have promised, you can do it as well without my company as with it, and I will remain here until you return."

The youth had not heard the almost noise-less tread of a powerful man who had followed close behind him since he entered the vaulted passage, and no sooner had he hesitated and refused to follow, than he was seized from behind and a handkerchief instantly drawn over his mouth. In vain was it that Alberte tried to resist, and in vain that he tried to raise an alarm, for he found himself within the grasp of a man who handled him as though he had been an infant; and after passing through several small passages, the creaking of a heavy bolt fell upon his ear. Not a word had yet been spoken, but as he was forced into a dark dungeon, which had been revealed by the opening of a heavy iron door, his stranger guide mockingly said—

"Now, boy, you may seek for the lordship of your father, and perchance you may yet win the lady Isidora's hand! Ha, ha, ha!"

Again and again that mocking laugh fell upon the ear of the youth, until at length all was silent as the grave.

Marino Trivisano had his dreaded enemy within his power, and his son had entrapped a dangerous rival!

THE BRAVO AT HIS CRUCIBLE.

CHAPTER IX.

Darkness and night—The thread of life is not yet to be severed—Isidora learns of Alberte's fate—Her reflections, and her strange visiter—Developments.

NIGHT was upon the soul of Alberte Lioni! All, all was night! The sun, the moon, the stars, all rolled on in their course, but they imparted to him no ray of their cheerful light. The hopes, the aspirations, the plans of the future, all sank in the utter darkness of despair, and around his heart wound the slimy viper of dull despondency. The fever came not again to warm his blood; the delirium came not to start forth the effervescence of his brain; but cold as ice ran the tide of life through his veins, and with a leaden weight sank the power of mental action. Those who fattened upon the wealth of his father had come to gloat over the fall of the son. He knew now that he was in the hands of the man who had occasion to fear him, and his young experience taught him that *fear* was the iron tyrant of despotism. To revenge, the soul of daring may look with boldness; but in the hands of a power which is actuated by that evil genius, Fear, there is no hope for mercy, no expectation of reprieve; 'tis the coward's main-spring of action, the strong foothold of Satan, and the only thing which will call forth the deadly sting of the insignificant viper.

Alberte kept no account of time, for in the darkness of his dungeon all minute-marks were but the continuous, undefinable portions of chaotic eternity, and the hours of the day and the hours of the night rolled alike over his soul, without the least indication from the great dial of nature to tell him when they commenced or when their end had come.

But the youth was not destined to a hasty death, for from an unseen hand he at length received a small allowance of coarse food. He heard the grating of a small wicket in the door of his cell, and he heard the sound of a basket, as the invisible bearer placed it upon the cold, damp pavement; he called aloud for an explanation of his strange confinement—he cried for mercy, but no voice answered his own; the iron wicket was closed, and again his own heart sent forth the only noise which broke the stillness of his prison. For a moment the thought flashed across his mind, that 'twere better to die at once than to be thus kept alive by a mercy which was cruelty in itself; but as this thought came, it brought with it a companion—the love of life; then came the demands of nature which God had given him for a monitor, and the youth groped his way to where the food had been placed. As he ate and drank, a portion of strength returned to its throne, and though he knew it not, still there was a faint hope struggling up in his bosom, and already it pointed its dim, waving finger upwards towards the Heaven of eternal justice.

Heavy was the sound which fell upon the ears of Isidora Vivaldi when she learned the first intelligence of her lover. The twilight had deepened into night, that night had given place to another day, and still he came not back; but at length a messenger returned and reported that the youth's gondola had been picked up far out in the Adriatic, where it was found with its bottom turned upwards. From early morn till late at night, the messengers of Vivaldi were upon the search, but not the slightest intelligence could be gained of the missing youth, further than the fearful tale which was told by the upturned gondola.

"He's gone—gone for ever!" uttered the fair Isidora, as her father vainly endeavored to quiet her. "My heart's best and only love lies beneath those very waters from whence, but a few short days ago, he so nobly rescued me. Be still, my soul! settle down, ye clouds of despair—the dream of years has passed, and I awake in the tomb of this life's joys!"

"But, my dear child," urged the old man, more stricken by the uncontrollable grief of his daughter than by the misfortune which had caused it, "there is yet no certainty of Alberte's death. Let not such deep misery weigh you down."

"Father," exclaimed the weeping girl, as she raised her eyes, and swept the tears for a moment from her face, "did you feel as I feel, you would not ask me to restrain my grief. I know not why it is, but this heavy blow seems but the presage of a heavier yet to come. I can see a dark cloud gathering above our house, and ere long it must send its lightning bolt upon us. This is but the rising of the terrible storm."

The lord Vivaldi talked long and earnestly with his daughter, but from the fearful thought which haunted her imagination he could not move her; and with a heart in which Isidora's forebodings had already called up slight misgivings, he at length left her apartment.

This was no sudden love that lay at the fountain-head of the fair girl's grief. He that has possessed an inestimable treasure, enjoyed its blessings, its hopes, its joys, and then lost it, prizes it doubly when kind fortune once more returns it to him. So it was with Isidora. Love's bright diadem had been worn in childhood—'neath Italia's warm clime her heart had realized the worth of the jewel, when it was lost. Once again, after the lapse of years, that jewel of the soul was found and worn; and when, the second time, it was lost, more keenly than ever fell the sharp blade of fate upon the tender chords of her joys. Then, again, the very doubt—if doubt it way be called—which hung over the prize—the hopes not yet realized, which depended upon the accomplishment of her lover's plans—lent a peculiar depth to the fervor of her love, and perhaps she felt more severely the blows, than she would had there been no doubts previous to the catastrophe.

For half an hour after her father left her, Isidora sat alone in her own chamber. She tried to analyze the feelings that stirred in her soul; she sought to solve the fears that oppressed her brain; but nought, save the one reality—the loss of Alberte—could she bring within the ken of her mental vision. Suddenly she felt an impression steal over her that she was not alone—she thought she heard the pulsations of a heart besides her own, and turning round, her eyes rested upon a form which was familar to her sight. At any other time she would have been startled by so summary an intrusion upon her privacy, but at the present time a quick thrill of something like hope trembled upon her thoughts, as she saw the most powerful man of all Venice gazing intently upon her. If there was a person in the commonwealth who had the power to aid her, that person was surely NICCOLI, the chief spy of the Council of Ten; and he it was who now stood in her presence!

"Lady," said the spy, as he laid his hand upon her shoulder, "you know me too well to wonder at my strange intrusion; and, hence, I will at once to the business that brought me hither, for I see by the dial upon St. Mark's, that the sun has already passed its meridian, and I must be brief. I know that one whom you loved has gone, and I know, too, how sudden was his disappearance; but whether you have loved him wisely or not, remains yet to be seen."

"Oh, sir," exclaimed Isidora, "he was kind and noble; his heart was pure and uncontaminated by the vices of the city; his only fault in the eyes of the world was his misfortune. Tell me, sir, do you know aught of his fate?"

"Not yet, fair lady; but if you can answer me a simple question, I may possibly gain some clue to his whereabouts."

"Name it, sir—name it."

"Do you know if Carolus Trivisano felt any ill-will towards him?"

"If he knew of his affection for me," returned Isidora, "he would be sure to, for even towards me he has used threats."

"Very well. At what time did the young man leave the palazzo yesterday?"

"I looked upon yonder dial, sir, just as his boat put off, and I remember distinctly that the shadow fell upon the hour of two."

"Of this you are sure."

"Yes, sir," replied Isidora; and then, looking imploringly into the stern countenance of Niccoli, she continued—

"Now, tell me, sir, if I have any grounds for hope?"

"Hope, fair lady, is a fickle thing," returned the spy, as he regarded his companion with a look of tender compassion. "It will not sustain the life which often clings so confidingly to it. Alberte Lioni may still live, and I may yet save him from the fate which had been assigned for him; but I would have you prepare for the worst, for be assured that darker clouds than you have yet seen are gathering over you."

"So my own soul has taught me to fear. But you, who know all the secrets of Venice, can surely guard me against them."

"Ah, lady, you know little of Venice. I can read the actions of men, but their thoughts are not mine. Evil lives in the heart, and there are hearts about you which contain the germs of all the evil you have to fear; those hearts beat only within the darkness I cannot penetrate. All that I know I will tell you; not for the sake of sounding in your ears a tale which shall fill your bosom with fear, but that you may be prepared to expect the blow ere it comes. There is a dread blow aimed at the government of Venice, and if it be not averted, the house of Vivaldi will come among the first of its victims. Isidora Vivaldi, can you hear the worst?"

"Go on, sir—go on. Let me know all; but for the love of Heaven, do not deceive me."

"Then, I fear that the fate of Alberte Lioni is worse for you than would have been his death. The youth is leagued with conspirators. Revenge for his father's wrongs has stirred up his soul to rebellion, and in the hands of artful men he has been made the tool of conspiracy. If such be indeed the case, the hands of justice will fall heavily upon him."

"Oh no, sir," exclaimed Isidora, in almost frantic accents; "Alberte could never do that. There is not a thought in his heart against the city of his birth. Oh, do not—do not haunt me with such terrible suspicions."

"I would not haunt you, lady, but there are stubborn facts in the way. Several times has he been seen in close conversation with the most dreaded man in Venice—he who eludes my grasp as though he were air— Marco Martelino. It was that fearful Bravo who so promptly rescued him from the death which threatened him upon the canal, and since then he has sought the youth even within his sick chamber. It was another hand that led him off yesterday, but even that hand is red with conspiracy. I have traced every circumstance, and now that I am sure at what time he left your father's palazzo, I can keep my eye upon him."

"And was it for this, sir, that you sought me?" bitterly exclaimed Isidora, as she turned her flashing eyes upon the spy. "Was it that from my evidence you might convict him? Oh, if it were treason to have shielded him from your power, then in Isidora Vivaldi you might have found another traitor. I tell thee that Alberte Lioni is innocent of any such crime, and in this bosom, at least, he shall ever find a heart that holds him honorable and true."

Was that a tear which glistened in the eye of the powerful Niccoli? Can that heart, so schooled in the criminal court of Venice, feel sympathy with a weeping girl? At least, the quick glance of Isidora caught the trembling of his dark lids, and she saw a bright drop start forth. She would have taken occasion to appeal to a sympathy which she thought must have arisen, but in a moment that countenance resumed its expression again, and as the spy turned towards the dial of St. Mark, he said—

"Think not too hard of me, lady, but rather school your heart for the truth, which, sooner or later, must fall like a thunderbolt upon it. I tell thee truly, that the blow must come. If, after that, you can rest upon a hope in the future, then so let it be. You may withstand the fearful storm, and yet ride safely in the haven of your hope's fruition."

As he spoke, Niccoli turned and left the apartment. Isidora heard his heavy footfall as he descended the broad stairs, and when at length all was silent, she turned her mind upon what had just passed. What could it mean? Long and earnestly she thought upon the strange revelations of the spy, but not a ray of light could she gather from the interview. It had been all surmise and suspicion, and to her all was doubt and fear. She did not believe that her lover was guilty of any crime, but she knew too well the fearful character of the power which hung over him, not to know that he was in danger, Then there was something more; her father was in danger, and she knew not even from what quarter to look for the evil. She was like the exposed wanderer in the midst of Heaven's flaming artillery—she knew not which portion of the dark cloud contained the bolt that was destined for her bosom.

CHAPTER X.

A friend in disguise—A dilemma with but one horn—A strange revelation—Alberte's temptation to conspiracy, and his noble answer thereto—The fearful oath—The Bravo's secret.

THE third basketful of food had been passed in to Alberte Lioni, and from this he judged that three days had dawned and set upon his strange confinement, for the third mess had been all eaten. As yet he had not heard a syllable from other lips than his own, nor had he seen the least glimmer of light. He was sitting upon a low pallet, which he had found in one corner of the cell, sadly meditating upon his hard fate, when he was startled by the grating of the small bolt which secured the wicket of his door. He knew that many hours would have to elapse ere the regular time for his food came round, and this was the first interruption he had received from any other source since his incarceration; but he had no chance for further reflection, for directly his ears were saluted with the inquiry, in a low tone—

"Is there any one here?"

"Yes," replied the prisoner.

"Lioni?"

"Yes."

The stranger made no further inquiry, but in a few seconds Alberte heard the low creaking of the heavier bolts, as they were withdrawn from their sockets; the door then slowly opened, and a light from a darkened lantern, not strong enough to blind him by its rays, sent the first cheerful gleams athwart his dungeon that had blessed his dreary solitude. He who held the lantern was so thrown in the shade, that our hero could not distinguish his form or features, but as he entered within the cell, he asked—

"Are you able to walk?"

"A short distance, at least," replied Alberte.

"Then follow me."

"But whither!"

"To liberty."

"How may I know it?"

"If you prefer to stay, I will again lock your door," laconically replied the visitor.

"No, no; anything is preferable to this, even death itself. I will follow you."

"Quickly, then," said the guide, as he turned to leave the place, "but make no noise."

The stranger took a different course from that which had been pursued in visiting the place, keeping directly on towards the end of the vaulted passage. When he reached the wall, he took from his girdle a small iron pin, which he inserted into a small puncture in the rock, and a large stone, which seemed to form the base of the arch, slowly swung inward, revolving upon two stout pivots fixed at the end. Through the opening thus formed the unknown guide easily passed; and when Alberte looked through, his eyes were greeted by the bright ripple of the moon-lit waters. A new life shot through his veins as he caught the welcome view; the fresh air came up like the invigorating breath of Heaven, sending an electric impulse along the muscular lines of his frame, and with a quick bound he followed on after his liberator. As he stepped from the aperture, the stone resumed its place, and he found himself upon the curb of the deep basin in which the patrician gondolas were secured. Into one of the boats the guide stepped, turning, as he did so, to assist Alberte; but our hero felt too exhilarated to need assistance, and he lightly stepped over into the gondola. The light of the moon dazzled his eyes a little, but not enough to prevent his seeing, and as the boat was shoved out from the basin, he had an opportunity to examine the man who had brought him thus far out of his bondage; but he made nothing from the observation, for the stranger was not only masked, but from the peculiar anomalies in his garments, Alberte was satisfied that he was deeply disguised. His short cloak was that of a senator, while his hat more nearly resembled the ducal bonnet than anything else—the hat giving the lie to the cloak, and the cloak utterly believing the rest of the dress. The youth would have asked a dozen questions which weighed on his mind,

but from the utter reserve of his companion he was led to infer that he would get no answer, at least till they left the canal; and he very wisely determined to remain quiet and await the result of his adventure.

The gondola swiftly glided down the smooth canal, passing beneath the shade of St. Mark's, along past the gorgeous palaces of the patricians, till at length it turned into one of the narrower streams which ran up among the casinos; and after a quick pull of several minutes, the powerful oarsman brought his boat to a sharp turn to the right, and drawing his oars quickly in-board, he bent his form slightly forward, and beckoned for Alberte to do the same. The bows of the gondola struck full upon the planking of a deep inlet from the canal; but instead of the sudden shock which the youth expected, he was surprised to see the wooden wall divide into two equal parts, and in a moment more he was gliding along in the midst of total darkness.

As the boat grated against the landing, the unknown removed the covering from his lantern, and as its dim rays struggled through the gloom, the youth found himself in what appeared to be the cellar of some large building, into which the waters of the canal had a free access. The guide stepped out upon the pavement, secured the boat, and then turning towards a flight of stone steps which led upward, he bade his companion follow him. Alberte did so with difficulty, for the way through several intricate turnings and narrow passages was dark, and he had hard work to keep up. He asked for no assistance, however, determined to remain silent till he should arrive at his journey's end. At length the wished-for moment arrived, for at the end of the last passage his guide unlocked a small door which opened to the left, and our hero was ushered into an apartment, which, if it was not large and sumptuous, was at least neat and comfortable, and no sooner had he reached a lounge, which stood beneath one of the balconied windows, than he settled upon its cushioned seat almost exhausted.

The unknown slowly turned the key upon the inside of the door, then walked to a table directly opposite to where Alberte had seated himself, and having lighted a wax taper, he removed his hat, cloak, and mask.

"The Bravo!" exclaimed Albert, starting up from his seat, as his eyes caught the dark features of the powerful man who led him thither.

"This is the second time that Alberte Lioni has owed his life to the dread of Venice," said Martelino, seeming not to notice the surprise of the youth; "but methinks you had rather be here than in the deep dungeons of the lord Trivisano."

"I have heard that it was you who saved me upon the canal, but till the present moment I have had no chance to return you my thanks; now, however, I do so most heartily, and I am sorry to be obliged to add, that for the present that is all with which I can repay you, but the time may come when I can assist you in turn."

"The time *has* come," replied the Bravo; "and for that reason I brought you hither, instead of leaving you with the lord Vivaldi."

"And what can I do for you?"

"Do you remember the wrongs of your father?" asked Martelino, as he narrowly watched the features of the youth, to see what effect his words would have.

"Do you suppose I can ever forget them, sir?"

"Not if you be a worthy son, certainly," replied the Bravo; and then gazing more intently than before, he continued—

"But have you the courage to revenge those wrongs?"

"Through the path of honor? yes!"

Martelino seemed somewhat disconcerted by this laconic answer; but without removing his fixed gaze, he continued—

"Do you not look upon the government which so justly condemned him as unholy and tyrannical in the extreme?"

"The agencies through which the deed was done were certainly infamous, but I cannot impute it all to the government."

"You are too lenient, my young friend. You know not how soon you may fall into the clutches of the same power. Now, if you have the courage to take up your father's cause, and stand boldly forth for the station to which your birth entitles you, you will be sure to find a host of friends with you. Let the present government be but once overturned, and you may yet ascend to the place you covet."

Alberte Lioni was startled by this bold proposal; and for some time he gazed wonderingly at his interlocutor without speaking. At length he asked—

"And would you have me turn traitor?"

"If for the down-trodden to seek the overthrow of their persecutors be treason, then I answer yes."

"Marco Martelino!" answered Alberte, while the rich blood filled the blue channels about his temples, "I feel a conscious pride in knowing that my father was innocent of the crime for which he was condemned; a thrill of joy runs through my frame, proscribed though my family name may be, when I reflect upon the fact that a traitor's blood runs not through my veins; and the honor which I inherited from one of the best of parents shall never be tarnished by me. No, sir; Giovanni Marcello loved Venice with his whole soul, and his son loves her equally as well. That son inherits not even the name of his father, but he does inherit from him a soul above treason, and that inheritance shall never pass from him. You have my answer."

While Alberte spoke, the sickly shade of his countenance was gone, the weakness of his frame was overcome, and his whole bearing was changed. A noble fire shot forth from his eyes, his limbs were nerved with the strong thongs of conscious right, and his soul struck boldly out into the sea of duty, regardless of the storms which might rise in the way. As he closed, that stern Bravo turned away, and sought the high window; his broad chest heaved with a peculiar emotion; and when at length he turned his face once more towards the light, there was a change so sudden and so strange, that Alberte scarcely realized that he gazed upon the fearful Bravo. Those piercing eyes were softened by the gentle dews of sympathy; those hard features were lighted by a look of kind gratitude; that towering form seemed shaken by the pulsations of a kindly-beating heart; and extending his hand to his young companion, he exclaimed—

"Go on in the path you have so nobly chosen, and far be it from me to attempt again to lead you astray. I have had wrongs which you know not of. Your father, young man, was not the only one who was banished from Venice—he was not the only one upon whom the foul wrong was done. I—I was banished, and I swore—aye, boy, deeply swore, and that oath is registered in Heaven—that I would be revenged. They may hunt the Bravo till the senate topples upon its foundation, the powerful all-seeing and subtle Niccoli may use all his art, and set his legions upon my track, but as sure as there is a Heaven above us, Marco Martelino will be revenged!"

Alberte Lioni gazed in rapt wonder upon the strange man before him; and though his oath was so fearful, still he could not help admiring the deep power of the soul which gave that oath a being, nor could he avoid sympathizing with the wrongs he had suffered. There was something in the looks of the Bravo which put a strange confidence in the bosom of the youth, and in a frank and open manner he said—

"I do not wonder, sir, that you seek for revenge, and if your revenge can mend the wrongs you have suffered, may God aid you in its pursuit; but for my own part revenge would not help me in the least—it would neither benefit myself, nor could it benefit my father. But are you not laying yourself liable to still greater suffering—perhaps an ignominious death—by the course you are pursuing?"

"No, boy," answered the Bravo, as he cast a peculiar look upon his companion's slight, but yet noble form. "The powers of Venice dare not take my life. At this moment there be thousands of strong hands in the city which would avenge my death. I have a SECRET, young man—a secret, the revelation of which would make Venice stir from its circumference to its very centre. Ah, I am well armed for the fight I have chosen, and ere another week the senate and council will begin to tremble beneath the strokes of my direful revenge. But I must leave you now, for I am needed. In yonder room you will find a bed, and upon the table are cordials and viands, and methinks the sooner you seek your rest the better. To-night and to-morrow you will spend beneath my roof, but after that I shall claim no further control over your actions. And now, my young friend, when Venice shall ring with the fearful deeds of the Bravo, I trust that in you he may at least find a heart that can sympathize with his wronged feelings, if not with his terrible deeds."

As he spoke, he threw the cloak over his shoulders, and placing the hat in which we first saw him, with the large black plume floating darkly from its side, upon his head, he left the apartment.

Alberte Lioni studied long and deeply upon the character of the strange man who had left him; and after he had sought his pillow, the dark, towering form still haunted him; but ere he could recall half the incidents that preyed upon his imagination, he fell into a dreamy, troubled sleep.

CHAPTER XI.

The conspirators once more—The new initiates, and their oath—The Bravo's cutting sarcasm— The plot made known to the plotters—The pledge of murder—The chemist at his crucible—The fatal compound—The sleeper and the spirit of evil—The shroud of death.

WHEN the Bravo left the place to which he had conveyed Alberte, it was nearly midnight, and as he stepped forth upon the pavement—for now he went on foot—he took his way towards the palace of Trivisano. He walked with long and quick strides, and ere many minutes he stood within the place where we have seen him before with the conspirators. They were all there, and the deep gloom, which a single taper could not dispel, cast a peculiar shadow over their features. There was more of fearfulness in their contracted brows than we have yet seen, and ever and anon, as they cast their furtive glances about from one to the other, they seemed to dread in each an enemy. A dark, meaning smile rested upon the face of Martelino as his eye ran over the trembling nobles, and his lips curled with a sneer; but none noticed it, for their plot was thickening about them, and its results and sequences were soon to tell how went it with them; their deeds could not much longer rest under cover of the darkness, and save the single purpose for which they were now collected, their whole attention was now turned to the events of the uncertain future.

The lord Marino Trivisano sat by a table upon which burned the only taper in the room, while under his elbow lay a parchment —the same that he was preparing when he was so unceremoniously interrupted by the spy—and this was the only instrument upon which their hopes of safety rested, in case their plot should be discovered. It was a false plan of conspiracy, purporting to have been drawn up by two of the most influential senators, to which had been forged the signatures of some half-dozen of the nobility; and this was to be placed in the private department of the man whose name stood first upon its face.

"Now," said Trivisano, as the Bravo took a seat, "let us at once initiate the new comers. From the senate we have Mentoni and Cordino, and from the procurators of St. Mark we have Floradi and Steffani. The latter is a most fortunate acquisition, for he has much influence with the keeper of the arsenal, and the whole armory may be easily taken possession of."

The light was extinguished, and after all had been arranged, the waiting nobles were brought in, one by one, and placed under the bans of the league. They were bound by the most fearful oaths which could be invented, to remain true to the interests of all concerned in the plot; and they were to lend every assistance in their power towards the overthrow of the senate and council; when the signal might be given, they were to head such of the people as might be seduced to join them; and, above all, they were to avoid the least sign of recognition in public till the final blow should be struck. When the oath was administered, and freely taken, the bandages were removed from their eyes, and the secrets of the conclave were theirs. Once more the taper was lighted, and the conspirators all turned their eyes upon the Bravo.

"Now, Martelino," said the lord Marino, "we have to do with thee."

"Say on, my lord," returned the Bravo.

"The lord Francis Vivaldi must not live to see the light of another sun!"

At the mention of the name of the chief of the senate inquisitors, and at the idea of such a sudden disposition of him, the newly-initiated nobles blanched and trembled.

"Perhaps you had not expected such summary measures," sarcastically remarked the Bravo, as he glanced at their trembling features.

"But the old inquisitor is powerful and popular," returned Mentoni, "and his removal will create more sensation than methinks the bud of a plot should warrant."

"You need not tremble for that," said the Bravo, "for Marco Martelino stands alone in the light. You may plot, my masters, to your heart's satisfaction, and your murders I will take upon my own hands, while I openly proclaim to all Venice what I have done; but you must do all but the killing—remember that."

"You are ready with your stiletto, sir Bravo," remarked Steffani, as he gazed with wonder upon the man of whom all Venice stood in dread.

"While others are equally ready with a traitorous brain," retorted Marco.

The hand of Steffani sought his dagger, but the meaning smile upon the lip of the man who had thus touched him, recalled him to himself, and he felt half-ashamed of the feeling he had betrayed; then turning to Trivisano, he remarked—

"I suppose, my lord, that you have all matters thus far safely arranged, and from your experience we may hope for a judicious arrangement to the end?"

"With you, my lord Steffani," returned the old noble, "rests your own safety, and if you are discreet you need not fear from others. Each man's own love of life must be his Mentor."

"And his ambition his leading star," quietly remarked the Bravo.

"Say, rather, his love of liberty," interrupted Castello, "for it is that alone which we seek."

"Aye, my lords and masters, so does the vulture seek for liberty, to prey upon whom it pleases, and when it pleases."

"And is not Martelino one of us?"

"Aye—for revenge, not for ambition."

"A distinction without a difference," said Castello; and as he noticed that the continuation of such a debate might create difficulty, he quietly pocketed his share of the cutting sarcasm, and then, turning to Trivisano, he continued—

"Come, my lord, let us have the arrangements you have made as soon as possible, that we may be studying upon the plans."

"Then you shall have them, as far as it has yet been practicable to arrange them. In two weeks from to-night, the senate, with the Doge and the six *savi* at its head, meet with the great council, and at that time the blow is to be struck. Within the suburbs there are three hundred men upon whom we can count for that night, and it will take them but a few moments to overcome the lords and nobles in the senate chamber. Dolfino, with a guard of six men, will be stationed at the entrance to the arsenal, and the moment the nobles are disposed of, our men will all rush to his assistance, and arms will be distributed to such of the citizens as will take sides with us. Martelino has asked to figure in the senate, and his arm alone will accomplish much, for it is there that he seeks revenge. The rope to the great bell of St. Mark will be cut, and from Steffani we must expect much aid in that quarter."

"That you shall have," returned Steffani, "and I may moreover promise you the assistance of some forty of the attendants."

"So fares the work well," said Castello, "Ah, there will be no need of brave hearts in the work when once the ball begins to roll, for the people of Venice are ripe for any change which is not for the worse."

"Be patient, my lords, be patient," said Trivisano, "for there is no danger of our failing. Now, Martelino, what say you, shall Vivaldi leave the earth to-night?"

"You have said it, and it shall be done," replied the Bravo. "But remember," continued he, while he looked hard upon Trivisano, "we war not upon defenceless females."

"What means that?" asked the noble, who seemed startled by the manner of Martelino.

"It means this, my lord: that if, by removing the father, I take the prop from the daughter, no hand shall do her harm. I think you understand me."

Whether Trivisano felt angry or not, he

ALBERTE SUMMONED BEFORE THE INQUISITION.

did not show it; but the nervous twitching of his muscles told plainly that he withheld some words which, had they been alone, might have found utterance. He looked upon the Bravo as far below him in rank, station, and power; but he knew, too, that in the work they had in hand they must be equals. A worm or a beggar he would have spurned, but he dared not awake the wrath of the tiger; so, with a bite of his thin lips, the lord Marino bowed to the will of the Bravo, in appearance, at least, and, with a forced look of friendly care, he said—

"Haste thee to thy work, Marco, for already has the morn of a new day sprung from the dead midnight, and you will be safer at the task now than in a few hours hence."

The Bravo bowed to Trivisano a silent answer, and, with a nod of parting farewell to the remainder of the assembly, he left the apartment.

As the Bravo emerged from the palace of Trivisano, he retraced his steps towards the house where he had left Alberte Lioni, and entering by a private way, he ascended to a small room, so situated at one extreme angle of the building, that no one would ever have noticed it, had not they previously known of its existence. The pressure of a small spring, which was adroitly inlaid with the bevel of the panel, caused the before-unnoticed door to open, giving admittance to a small room of crescent-shape, which it took from the swell-corner of the structure within which it was built. Within this apartment stood a small cabinet, from the front of which descended a writing-table, while in the upper part was a receptacle for books, manuscripts, &c. In one of the extremities of the room, where the meeting of the two walls formed a very acute angle, there was built a small furnace, within which a quantity of combustible materials was ready placed for immediate use, and as soon as Martelino had lighted a candle, he proceeded at once to ignite it. After watching for a few moments, to satisfy himself that the fire thus created would be sufficient for present purposes, he turned himself to the cabinet, and took a seat at the leaf; then unlocking a small drawer, he took therefrom an old vellum manuscript, and was soon buried in the depths of its mysteries.

As he sat thus, intently poring over the curious characters upon the parchment, the candle threw a deathlike glare upon his dark features, casting a strange, ominous look over his person, which loomed up in the slightly-relieved darkness like a dread spirit of evil. Ever and anon, as some passage would seem to strike his attention a grim smile of satis-faction rested for a moment upon his features, but it would quickly pass away, and again he would turn over the leaf and seek further. At length he gazed longer than before, line after line he read over, then re-read it, and with an exclamation of peculiar satisfaction he rose from his seat. Another key was placed in the case above his head, and as a small door swung open, the eye rested upon an arrangement of vials and boxes, variously and curiously labelled.

"Ah, thou faithful drugs—thou liquids of no color, smell, nor taste, save that which doth enchant, while yet thou windest thy subtle folds with deadly power about the heart—what treasures lie not in thy mystic depths! Thou, sweet-smelling drug, when all alone, can do no harm—a child might toy with thee from morn till night; and thou, smooth vial, might pour thy contents o'er an infant's tongue, and the doating mother should never weep that one so dear had tasted of thy limpid fluid. And thou, and thou, and still another. Ah, how weak and harmless are ye now, when thus divided from each other! and yet the soul of science takes thee in her hand, and lo! thou standest forth an enemy, which all the powers of earth may never conquer."

Thus mused the Bravo to himself, as he held a small crucible in his hand, within which he first placed a grain of drug, and then, referring to the manuscript at various intervals, he dropped in upon it a small portion of liquid from each of four vials. When this was done, the crucible was placed upon the furnace, and pressing a napkin hard upon his mouth and nose, the Bravo watched with eager eyes the heating of the compound. When his lungs had reached their utmost tension, he would slip to a small window— the only one in the room—and having taken breath, once more resume his watch over the furnace. At length the liquid began to boil, sending forth a pale yellow vapor, which rose in a cloud to the ceiling, where it hung like a death-pall. After it had thus boiled for several moments, a small ivory ball, containing a slight air-chamber, was dropped into the crucible, but it quickly sank; another and another followed, till the fourth, when a smile of satisfaction rested upon Marco's features, as the little white tell-tale floated upon the surface of the liquid. In a moment the compound was taken from the fire and poured into a small vial, which was stopped perfectly tight, and then deposited in the Bravo's bosom. In a short time the vapor swept out at the window, and Marco Martelino breathed much freer, as the dangerous power he had conjured up was thus subdued.

The lord Francis Vivaldi slept soundly in his bed; no thought of wrong sent his mind in the startling path of harrowing dreams, no pent-up feelings of evil disturbed the quiet of his peaceful slumber; but calmly he lay, like a good old man, as he was, nor dreamed he that the spirit of evil was so near. He heard not the slow, cat-like tread that seemed to come from the very wall; he heard not the slow click of steel, as a secret spring was started from its rest; he heard not the moaning sound, as a panel at the head of his bed was moved easily back from its place; nor saw he the towering form of the Bravo, as that fearful man stood within his room.

Slowly and silently did Marco Martelino approach the bedside of the sleeping noble, and a strange light rested upon his dark features, as he bent over his victim.

"This is the first blow for my masters," muttered the Bravo, while a dark frown gathered upon his brow, "but for thee, old man, it shall be an easy one. Sleep on, for when thou wakest again, thine eyes shall open in a place where enmity can harm thee not."

Marco drew the small vial from his bosom pocket, and having poured a few drops of the liquid upon the corner of a linen napkin, he gently held it to the nose of the sleeper. The old noble's left arm, which had been lying across his breast, gradually slipped off, until it rested powerless at his side; the eyes seemed to roll beneath the closed lids, as though they would have thrown off the drowsy power; and the muscles of his face trembled like the chords of a harp. Still that dark man pressed the fatal napkin closer and closer to the channel of breath, while with the fore-finger of his left hand he felt carefully for the pulsations of the weakening heart. At length there came a deep heaving of the chest, one heavy throe in the throat, a slight relaxation of the muscles about the face, and the heart of the lord Vivaldi was as quiet as the grave!

One old servant, who slept in the lower part of the building, thought he heard a heavy tread within the wall next to his bed, and in a moment more the sound of a shutting door, which he had never before heard, struck upon his ear. He sprang from his low couch, and just as he reached the window which overlooked the canal, he saw a gondola put quickly out from the basin. It was pulled by a powerful man; and as the moon sent her rays upon the scene, the old servant saw a form, covered by a large cloak, lying across the seats in the stern. As he gazed upon that cloak, now growing indistinct in the distance, something told him that it was the shroud of death!

CHAPTER XII.

Consternation of the people—The efforts of the spy to detect the murderer—The messenger—The Council of Ten in session—The strange epistle from the Bravo—Niccoli's revelation and the consequence.

THE next morning after the scene we last recorded, the intelligence of the lord Vivaldi's strange and sudden disappearance was circulated through the city; and the affair was of a character to create the most intense excitement, for the old noble had ever been a favorite with the people; not only from his true moral worth, but also from the vast influence which he exerted in their favor; consequently, on every hand, the bereaved household found ready and helping sympathizers. Niccoli came at once to the work of hunting up the mystery, and in less than an hour after he had received the intelligence, every nook and corner of Venice was being searched by one or more of his emissaries.

It might have been an hour and a half after Niccoli had first heard of the old noble's disappearance—not more than that, for the sun had scarce yet peeped over the house-tops —when he returned to his dwelling, for the purpose of making further arrangements for the prosecution of the business he had in hand. He had but just seated himself before a private cabinet, within which were elaborate records of all the criminal transactions in Venice, together with an accurate description of the criminals and their various places of rendezvous, when he was suddenly interrupted by the entrance of a messenger from the ducal palace.

"How now, Frederic?" exclaimed the spy, as he caught the flurried expression upon the messenger's countenance; "are the people in the palace stirring so soon?"

"Yes, Niccoli; the Ten are already in session, and they desire your attendance at once."

"Dost know their business?" asked Niccoli, as he placed his keen dagger in his bosom and buckled on a heavy sword of the finest Milan steel.

"No, sir," replied the youth, "I heard not at the council chamber; but in the street I learned that the old patrician Vivaldi had been murdered; and I think that must be the business they have in hand, for they all looked much troubled, and throughout the palace all was confusion and dismay."

In a few moments Niccoli was on his way; and when he entered the hall where the Ten held their secret sessions, he found them in deep and earnest consultation. The moment he closed the door behind him, the chief of the Ten immediately addressed him—

"Niccoli, dost know the deed that has been perpetrated within the night past?"

"If you mean the disappearance of the lord Vivaldi—yes."

"That is the matter to which I allude," returned the chief. "Have you yet done anything for the apprehension of the murderer?"

"We know not yet that he has been murdered," said the spy.

"But we do know that he has been most foully murdered, Niccoli, and his murderer must be arrested. Have you guarded the avenues leading from the city?"

"They are always guarded."

"Always?"

"Yes, my lord," returned Niccoli. "Not a man can leave Venice by night or day, the fact of which I cannot learn by asking."

"Then, has Marco Martelino left the city since the last setting of the sun?"

"No, sir."

"You are sure, then?"

"As I am that I stand here," returned the spy. "Over an hour and a half ago I had messengers in every part of Venice, and before I came here I heard from them all. Upon the daring Bravo I have had the most scrutinizing watch kept for a month back; and though he has thus far eluded my grasp, still I know of all his movements—or, at least, enough to assure me that he is in the city."

"It was he who committed this fearful murder."

"Martelino?"

"Yes."

"And how did you learn a fact which has been kept from me and my legions?" asked the spy, in astonishment.

"From the murderer's own lips."

"But surely you have not seen him? He has not dared—"

"No, no," interrupted the chief of the Ten, "he has not dared to show his person here; but for that matter he has dared enough.

Here is a letter which the Doge received this morning, and which he instantly laid before us. Read it, Niccoli."

The spy took the letter, and turning to the light, he read as follows:—

"To Francesco Dandolo, Doge of Venice, and Cancellieri, the chief of the Ten:

"To-day's sun will rise upon the corpse of Francis Vivaldi. Venice has lost her chief Inquisitor. The old noble has fallen first, but there are more yet whose lives are forfeited. This is the first blow I have struck to avenge the wrongs received at your hands; and though all the city is in tumult from this one death, yet Venice itself shall tremble, ere there be empty seats enough in your senate to glut the revenge of

"Marco Martelino."

Niccoli read the strange epistle over the second time, and then turned slowly towards him from whose hands he had received it. There was a bright, fiery spot in either eye, and the nether lip trembled and turned pale.

"What thinkest thou now?" asked the chief, as he received back the Bravo's daring letter.

"I think as I have ever thought, that Marco Martelino is to be feared; and there is no doubt that, if he be not apprehended, he will carry his threat into execution."

"If he be not apprehended? He must be apprehended," exclaimed Cancellieri, with much vehemence.

"I know that he should be," returned Niccoli, "but thus far every effort to that effect has failed; though, in truth, I have not tried so much to take him, as I have to watch his movements, for, upon my honor, I believe that he has powerful aid at his back."

"I know that he has so intimated," said the chief, "but he has evidently done that to distract our aim. Let every means in your power be put at once into requisition, and if the Bravo be alive, and within Venice, he must be taken."

"Your wishes shall be obeyed," replied the spy. "Already I have my eye on a person from whom I think we may gain some intelligence. He is a young man, and I have every reason to believe that he is an accomplice of the Bravo, for on more than one occasion have they been seen together, and only last night they rode in company upon the canal."

"But of one thing tell me," interrupted the chief. "How is it that this fearful man, this scourge of Venice, is so often seen, even upon our canals, and yet he cannot be taken? There must be some strange mystery here."

"And so there is, my lord; a mystery which I cannot fathom. He disappears from view with a facility equalled only by the fairy tales of the enchanted cap. Sometimes his boat seems to glide clean through the very walls of the canal; and again you may follow him in the street, and at the first approach towards his person he will glide into some narrow passage and is nowhere to be found."

Cancellieri mused long upon the words of the spy, and at length, raising his head, he asked—

"And what of this accomplice? Who is he?"

"Do you remember Giovanni Marcello?"

"Yes."

"He was banished on suspicion of treason."

"On conviction of treason," said the chief of the Ten.

"Very well; he was banished, and you gave his son permission to return to Venice."

"As a student and a common citizen: yes."

"But took away his family name?"

"Certainly."

"He is known as Alberte Lioni."

"Well."

"And Alberte Lioni is an accomplice of Marco Martelino."

"Ha! and has treason grown in the child, too?" exclaimed the chief. "Can you take him, Niccoli?"

"I can, my lord."

"Then let him be brought before us ere the sun goes down; and, if needs be, set every citizen in Venice upon the track of the Bravo."

Niccoli bowed respectfully to the council, and in a few moments he was in the street. People gazed in wonder upon the spy, as he walked by, and instinctively did they turn out to let him pass. In him they looked for the man who was to cope with the terrible Bravo!

CHAPTER XIII.

Fate once more grows dark—The spy and his prisoner—The hall of the Inquisition—The questioning—Base falsehoods of the patrician witnesses—The fearful rack is unstrung—Sudden interruption of the spy, and its result.

ALBERTE LIONI rose from his bed late in the morning, and for some time the events of the preceding night floated dimly through his brain; but at length he gained a clear idea of what had passed, and now, as much as before, was he in doubt with regard to the disposition which was to be made of him. The door of his room he found open, but the one beyond—that which he had at first entered—was closed against his egress; and while he meditated upon the strange fate which seemed to have dropped thus suddenly upon him, he proceeded to complete his toilet. He found plenty of food upon the sideboard, together with wines and cordials; and everything else about the place was calculated to have administered to the comfort of one who had a mind at rest; but at that moment Alberte Lioni would have been happier by far in the homeliest place upon the earth, so that he would have been a free man.

Ah! 'tis not what men call wealth that begets the happiness of life; 'tis not the goods of earth that minister to the health of humanity's soul; 'tis not the sumptuous palace, the gaudy trappings, the liveried servants, and the dainty viand, that create the joys of God's children here on earth, but 'tis the mind content with what it has. We may find contentment on a throne; still, who would think of looking for it there? Beneath the humble cot this jewel in the diadem of life glistens with a brighter effulgence, and oftener, too, than anywhere else.

Alberte ate of the food, because nature called for it, but had it been a crust of hard bread, it would have been all the same; he sat down upon a soft damask lounge, but had his body reclined upon a slab of granite, he would never have cared for the difference. He felt ill at ease, not only because he was ignorant of his own fate, but because there was another who would certainly weep for his absence. Then, too, where were his hopes of the future? where those bright pictures he had painted upon the canvass of imagination? and where the ground for his aspirations? He knew that enemies were upon his track, and that they aimed at his downfall; but why they sought to harm him he only knew from the remark of him who had first led him to the dark dungeon beneath the palace of Trivisano. From this he knew that he could not gain the property of his father without dispossessing some one else; and also that he could not possess the hand of Isidora without that property. A rival, too, perhaps he had, and a powerful one; and if such was the case, to what dangers might he not be exposed?

Such were the thoughts that passed through

the youth's mind, as he reclined upon the lounge; and while he dwelt upon the curious conduct of the Bravo, he was aroused by the heavy tread of many feet upon the stairs. Next came a crashing rap at the door; but before he could arise to ascertain the cause of the tumult, the door was burst open, and Niccoli, followed by half a dozen men, strode into the apartment. Alberte, who stood utterly confounded by this strange intrusion, had not the power to ask for an explanation, for upon the dark robes of those who followed the spy, his eye caught the fearful cypher which denoted the officers of the inquisition!

"Your name is Alberte Lioni," said Niccoli, as he approached.

"You are right," answered our hero.

"Then, officers, here is your prisoner."

"But, sir," exclaimed Alberte, as he turned an imploring gaze upon the spy, "tell me what I have done. Of what am I accused?"

Niccoli returned no answer, nor did he even stop to look at the supplicant, but turning quickly upon his heel, he left the place.

The unfortunate youth knew that it would be of no use to question those in whose power he was left, for their lips were ever sealed upon all subjects connected with their duty; so he submitted in silence to the mandate of the spy, and was led from the chamber.

Beneath that department of the ducal palace in which the Council of Ten held their usual sessions, there was a long, narrow room, dimly lighted by a single lamp, which hung from the ceiling, directly in front of a high chair—the chair being robed in black; and into this room was Alberte Lioni conducted by the officers who had taken him from the chamber of the Bravo.

A bandage, which had been placed upon his eyes, as soon as he reached the palace, was now taken off, and a cold chill crept through his veins, as his eyes ran over the place within which he stood. On one side of the room stood the high, black chair, surmounted by an iron arm, the hand of which grasped a bright sword—the whole representing justice! It was well that arm was of iron, for the justice symbolized by the sword which it bore was never known to bend from its purpose. Upon that cold, iron arm the angel of mercy would have found no resting-place. To the right of the chair, against the black partition, looking in the dim light like a gaunt spectre of death, stood the blood-stained rack, while around, upon every hand, were arranged the terrible appurtenances of the Venetian Inquisition!

No wonder that Alberte Lioni trembled, for men stouter than he had stood there before him, and trembled. Whatever may have been his feelings, as he gazed around, or whatever may have been the doubts that rose to his mind, they were all speedily ended by the entrance of the inquisitor of the lesser criminal court, who took his seat in the high chair; and after a few moments of private conversation with those who had brought the prisoner hither, he turned to Alberte, and asked—

"Do you know why you are brought hither?"

"No, sir—indeed I do not."

"Then you have not the least conception?"

"No, sir."

"If you were placed upon your oath, now, you could not tell why you are a prisoner?"

"Most assuredly not," answered Alberte, who was surprised at this continuous questioning upon a single point.

"Take that down," said the inquisitor, as he turned to the scribe at his side; and then, looking again towards the prisoner, who stood trembling before him, he continued—

"Can you tell me in whose apartment you were found by the officers?"

The youth hesitated a moment, ere he answered. The Bravo had saved his life twice, and he could not help feeling grateful; and besides, he had promised that whenever opportunity should offer, he would return the favor. Perhaps his answer might lead to Martelino's apprehension, and consequent death. Then again came the thoughts of duty. The man who saved his life was seeking the lives of others, and should his own knowledge be withheld, he might be indirectly an agent in the crime. But while he hesitated, the inquisitor had marked his manner, and in rather a sarcastic tone, he said—

"Perhaps we can help you to your memory, young man. Are you aware by whom you were conducted to your last night's quarters?"

"I am, sir," replied Alberte, who was now determined to answer every question, to the best of his knowledge.

"Who was it?"

"He is called Marco Martelino."

"Aha! you remember, then. Take that down, and mark the hesitation, secretary." Then turning to the youth, he continued—

"Are you aware of the character of this Martelino?"

"Only that he has been kind to me, sir; for twice has he saved my life."

"And did you know nothing of his intentions with regard to the State of Venice?"

"I knew, sir, that he meditated some deep revenge for wrongs which he had received."

"And you did not inform us of it. Mark that, secretary. Now, sir," continued the inquisitor, turning from the secretary to

Alberte, "tell us truly, and without hesitation, did you not know upon what business this Bravo was engaged when he left you last night?"

"No, sir."

"You had not the least idea of it?"

"Not the least."

"Then you know not that Marco Martelino, after he left you last night, murdered the lord Francis Vivaldi?"

"Murdered! Vivaldi!" exclaimed Alberte, while he trembled and turned ashy pale. "Great God of mercy, grant that this be false. Oh, sir, you do not mean that Vivaldi was murdered?"

"He was murdered, young man, and that, too, by the Bravo. But why do you feel such sympathy for him? Ah, your feelings betray the workings of a guilty conscience. You knew of this before."

"As I hope for a Heaven hereafter, sir, I did not. For the lord Vivaldi I felt the utmost respect and esteem; for beneath his roof, and fostered by his kind care, I recovered from a fearful illness. No, sir; God knows that this poor life of mine would willingly have gone out, had it been needed, in defending that of the old noble."

"If you loved him so well, methinks you should have staid beneath his roof; at least, until you had perfectly recovered."

"But I was basely decoyed away, sir, and confined within a dark dungeon."

"By the Bravo, I suppose?"

"No, sir," quickly returned Alberte; "I was dragged away by one of the nobles of Venice—the younger Trivisano—and by him and his father was I kept in a dark, damp dungeon beneath their palace."

"And from thence Martelino released you?"

"Yes."

"Have you got all down?" asked the inquisitor of the secretary.

"I have, sir," replied the latter.

"Then let the messenger be called."

In a few minutes the same youth who had summoned Niccoli to appear before the Ten entered the room, and the inquisitor, turning again to the secretary, said—

"Fill out a summons for the lord Trivisano and his son to appear upon the instant before our tribunal."

As soon as the instrument was ready, the inquisitor placed his signature to it, and affixed the large black seal of the office; then handing it to the waiting messenger, he bade him hasten with it to the palace of Trivisano.

Alberte was conducted to a seat, to await the arrival of those who had been sent for; and the inquisitor, after looking over the late records of the secretary, upon which he made several minutes of his own, busied himself in turning over a heap of papers which lay upon the table before him. The youth knew that Trivisano and his son had only been sent for as witnesses, for before this tribunal those of the patrician rank were never brought for aught else, and as he thought upon the events of the last few days, in connection with this, his heart sank within him. He had learned, as the reader already knows, how much he stood in their way, and if they had once tried to murder him by inches, in order to effect his removal, what might they not do now, when chance had placed within their power the means of merely perjuring his life away. Around him there were none to sympathize, and wherever he turned his eyes he met but the cold, hard features of those who regarded him as a criminal. Those dark-robed officers of Venetian justice had seen too many young men led from that hall to the scaffold, to feel much sympathy with youth and beauty; they were like the heavy cog-wheels of an engine, doing only what had been marked out for them, without regard to aught else. They did nothing but their prescribed duty; they knew nothing but that duty, nor cared or thought of anything but duty.

The dull and tedious moments rolled on, each seeming an hour to the heart-stricken youth, till at length Marino Trivisano and his son entered the hall. As the old noble walked towards the inquisitor's chair, his eyes rested upon Alberte Lioni, and instinctively he exclaimed—

"Holy mother! what is this?"

Carolus Trivisano caught the ejaculation of his father, and his own face blanched as he found the object of it. Had that father and son beheld the dark sovereign of Tartarus before them, they could not have been more astounded, for, until that moment, they thought Alberte Lioni safe within their own power. For a moment the old noble forgot that within this court the patrician could not be tried for any crime against the state, and a fearful tremor shook his frame, as the thought flashed across his mind that something had been discovered of his plot.

"You are perhaps astonished, my lord," said the inquisitor, as he noticed the old noble's perturbation, "to see that your prisoner has escaped. Did you not know before that he had gone?"

"Gone!" murmured the old man to himself; but recollecting himself in a moment, he replied—

"No, sir."

"Then it seems this terrible Bravo knows your house as well as others."

Again Trivisano gasped for breath; but he was quickly relieved by further remark from the inquisitor, who continued—

"This young man, called Alberte Lioni, has been brought hither under charge of being leagued with Marco Martelino. Niccoli has often seen them together, and this morning he was arrested in one of the Bravo's haunts. He informs us that Martelino rescued him from the dungeons beneath your dwelling, whither he was conveyed by your orders; and I have sent for you and your son, that we may come at the truth, for the prisoner himself is given to strange forgetfulness in his knowledge of the facts we would arrive at."

Now Trivisano breathed again, for the immediate fear was removed. Perhaps Martelino had played him false, but that lay further off; and immediately collecting his scattered senses, he replied, while a bold heartless look rested upon his features—

"The truth you shall have, sir inquisitor, though it would have pleased me better, had yonder youth remained longer under my roof. You are probably aware, sir, that— I believe there are no tattlers here?"

"No, sir," replied the master. "Not a word spoken here goes to other ears than the Ten."

"Then, sir, perhaps you are aware that I am authorized by the council to use such means, for the present, as I may see fit, for the apprehension of this Bravo, or any who may be connected with him."

"I know it, sir."

"Upon your prisoner," continued Trivisano, "I have for some time looked with suspicion; and at length I received positive information that he was plotting in the very household of the lord Vivaldi. I waited only till I was doubly sure of the truth of this, when I at once had him arrested through the agency of my son."

"What led first to your suspicions, my lord?"

"By learning that the Bravo visited him often, while he lay sick at Vivaldi's house."

"And, might I ask, what confirmed those suspicions?"

For a moment Trivisano hesitated; but his heart was too much schooled in duplicity to stick at any ordinary difficulty, and with the most perfect *sang-froid*, he replied—

"You must excuse me, sir, if, under the authority of my office, I decline to answer your question, for I have much at stake for the safety of Venice which may not now be known. Suffice it for me to say, however, that Alberte Lioni is an accomplice of Marco Martelino."

"Great God of justice, defend me from that base and heartless liar!" exclaimed the horror-stricken youth, as he heard that grey-headed old man utter such falsehoods against him.

"Silence!" almost shouted the iron master, between his set teeth. "Utter another word like the last, and the gag shall stop thy mouth." Then turning to Carolus Trivisano, he continued—

"Can you inform us of anything which your father has left unsaid?"

"Only one thing," replied the young noble, while he cast a triumphant look upon his rival. "On the day I captured him, I watched him for several moments engaged in earnest conversation with a powerfully-built man, who wore a large hat, over which floated a long black ostrich feather. They were in separate boats, and when the prisoner pulled his gondola towards me, I took him prisoner. From the description I have since had of the Bravo, I am confident that the person with whom Lioni was conversing must have been him."

Poor Alberte now felt indeed that his case was hopeless. In the rectitude of his own heart, he had not conceived it possible that any man could so unblushingly fabricate falsehoods of such monstrous magnitude and evil consequence as had just dropped from the lips of that father and son; but they had been told, and they had been heard—and, alas! they had been believed.

That cold iron arm seemed to tremble above the master's black chair, and the keen bright blade which it held seemed to incline its edge towards the ill-fated youth.

At the sign from the master, the two nobles left the place; and as soon as the door was closed, the former turned to Alberte with a threatening look, and said—

"Now, young man, let your answers be quick and to the point, or we shall find means to aid you in giving them. First, where is Marco Martelino?"

"Indeed, sir, I do not know."

"Where were you to see him again?"

"As true as there is a God who hears me, I know not that I should ever have seen him again."

"Then you persist in denying all knowledge of his whereabouts?"

"With the naked, ungarnished truth upon my lips, I do," returned Alberte, who began to be alarmed by the aspect of the inquisitor's countenance.

"But once more shall I trust to thine

LORD BLENZI ENTRAPPED BY THE MONK.

unaided memory to answer me," uttered the master, as he turned a meaning look upon his officers. "Will you, by any means in your power, give us the least knowledge of where the Bravo may be found?"

Alberte looked for several moments into the face of his questioner, and then, while a tear started from his eye, called up by the thought that none believed him, he answered, in slow and measured accents—

"That truth which has ever been my guiding star, has led me to all that I have said since I have been within these walls : and once more I tell thee, as God is my judge, I know no more of the present situation of Marco Martelino, nor of his arrangements for the future, than does the infant who lies unconscious upon its mother's breast. And, furthermore, every word which the lord Trivisano and his son have uttered concerning me is false—basely, cruelly false."

The master did not speak in answer to this, but he simply touched a small cord which hung down by the side of his chair, and in a few moments two men, robed in black, and wearing black masks upon their faces, entered by a small door in the further extremity of the room. As they approached the centre of the hall, the rays of the lamp fell upon their ominous forms, and revealed a large scarlet cross wrought upon each of their breasts. Alberte's eyes fell upon that bloody insignia, and the chill that thrilled in his veins waxed colder yet. Mechanically those two men moved towards the fearful engine that reposed, like a slumbering demon, at the end of the room, and while it creaked and groaned, as it woke from its rest, it was slowly wheeled to the front of the black chair. The blocks and the strong cords rattled forth a death-like sound, as it came to a stand, and Alberte saw before him the bloody rack !

The cold-hearted master of that dread apartment spoke not yet; but by a sign of the fore-finger he instructed his officers to proceed, and the two men, from whose breasts looked forth the red crosses, seized the youth by the shoulders, and threw him upon the rack. The cords were passed around his arms and around his ankles, the blocks were set ready for the stretch, and then the master said—

"Before your limbs are racked by the torturer, will you tell us of the Bravo?"

Alberte Lioni could have suffered in a good cause without a murmur; or had he aught to conceal which his honor bade him keep secret, he could have held his lips even unto death; but to be tortured thus without a cause— thus to be doomed, when all within his own heart was pure and innocent—was more than fortitude could bear, and in the agony of his breaking heart, he exclaimed—

"Oh, sir, for the love of Heaven, do not put me to the fearful rack. If you have one spark of mercy in your bosom, if one grain of justice be left in your power, torture me not; for if this heart could be torn from my breast, you would see it as innocent of crime as—"

"Enough, enough!" harshly interrupted the master. "Now, tell me what I would know. That look, those tears, will never move me. Let the wheel be turned!"

"Hold, there!" shouted a deep voice at the door, and as they gazed in the direction from whence it came, they beheld the Spy of the Ten advancing up the hall.

"How now, bold intruder?" said the master, while a flush of anger passed over his features. "How dare you thus intrude upon the secret tribunal of Venice?"

"Dare!" repeated the spy, with a contemptuous look. "I come with a power which Venice has made higher than thine or thy tribunal. Unbind that youth!"

"Hold!" exclaimed the master, as the men sprang obedient to the will of Niccoli. "That prisoner is mine till I have done with him."

"He may have been yours to question, but not to torture," returned the spy. "In the name of the Ten, I tell you once more to unbind him."

Again the dark-robed men laid their hands upon the cords, but instinctively they sought the gaze of their master at the same time; and as they found no token of resistance there, they proceeded with the work. The inquisitor felt angry that his authority fell to the ground before that of another, but against the Ten he dared not even murmur.

"Have you asked all the questions you desired?" inquired Niccoli, as Alberte was once more upon his feet.

"I have asked them all," rather sharply replied the master.

"That is enough."

So saying, Niccoli ordered two of the officers to lead the prisoner as he should direct, and in a few moments Alberte Lioni stood within the hall of the Council of Ten !

CHAPTER XIV.

Alberte before the Council of Ten—The prison-chamber, and its strange furniture—"What kind power has sent me this?"—A partial explanation from the spy—His mysterious words at parting.

AS our hero found himself in the presence of those ten men whose power could shake the senate, and to whose authority the Doge must bow in silence, he could not suppress the feeling of awe that crept over him. Even though he was before the most subtle tribunal in Venice, still the feeling of alarm and fright which the rack and its dark concomitants had created, seemed removed from his bosom, and in its place came the one sensation of awe-inspired dread. He dreaded the power from the decisions of which he knew there was no appeal—a power which he knew was final and unalterable. He dreaded without fright, without alarm; for the majesty of that mighty council overcame the immediate cause for fear which had sprung from the lesser court of the inquisition. The bold-hearted man will face, undaunted, death and terror in a thousand shapes, and yet tremble with fright at the touch of the almost insignificant scorpion.

The Council of Ten had but little to do with Alberte. They asked the same questions which the lesser inquisitor had put, and then gave him up to the sole charge of Niccoli. By the latter he was conducted to a place of close confinement, but it was not a dungeon, nor yet was it a dreary cell, though, in truth, it was a prison from whence to escape was utterly impossible. Through the grated windows the fresh breezes of Heaven blew in grateful zephyrs, and around the room were all the necessities of comfort. One thing was alone wanting, that sweetest blessing of life, liberty. In one corner of the room stood a table, and upon its surface, and by its side, were implements, the sight of which sent a thrill through the youth's frame. 'Twas the well-known easel, the palette, the brushes, the paints, and even the canvas of his long-neglected studio.

"What kind power has sent me this?" asked Alberte, as he gazed upon his conductor.

"'Twas one who loves thee, young man, even though dark suspicion rests upon thy name."

"I know of but one in Venice."

"Then it must have been that one."

"That is the daughter of him who was last night murdered," said Alberte, while a cold shudder passed over him.

"And she it was who sent them hither," answered the spy.

"She?—but how?—what time? Surely she did not think of this when her poor father is but just dead."

"She knew of your confinement yesterday," returned Niccoli; "or rather, she knew that you were to be confined, for she was informed of the suspicions we had against you; and when she learned that something might be done to relieve the tedium of your solitude, she begged that the implements of your cherished art might be your companions."

"God bless her!" fervently ejaculated the youth, as a tear started to his eye, and then turning to the spy, he asked—

"Does she believe me guilty of any crime?"

"Not yet."

"Then she never will, for she knows there dwells no thought of wrong within my heart. But tell me, sir, may I not write to her?"

"Anything that I can read."

"I thank you, sir—thank you heartily. I have not a thought that I would hide from the sympathizing heart of him who feels for the wrongs of others, nor have I a word to write that you may not study in every import."

One question more Alberte wished to ask, but he feared that he should get no answer. However, the kind manner of Niccoli thus far so emboldened him, that he determined to make the trial; and gazing imploringly into the face of his companion, he said—

"I have been twice taken prisoner; once by the son of lord Trivisano, in a most villanous and unaccountable manner, from whose power I was arrested by this dread Bravo, but for why I cannot tell; and now I am taken by yourself. May I not know what it all means?"

"I will tell you as much as I can," replied the spy, "for I have certainly no desire to rack you with useless suspense. Why, the lord Trivisano and his son have sought thee, you may know as well as I, for they have only told me what you heard them tell the master of the lesser inquisition."

"Aye, I do know," replied Alberte, while his eyes flashed. "They fear me—not for the state, but for themselves. I believe they know that the property and the power which they hold by public authority was unjustly confiscated, and they fear that I, if at liberty, might gain my rights. Hence the base falsehoods they have fabricated."

"Well," said the spy, without betraying either a sign of assent or disapprobation at the conclusions of the youth, "and have you no idea of what were Martelino's intentions in releasing you from the power of Trivisano?"

Niccoli had fixed his eyes calmly but yet sternly upon Alberte as he asked the question, and without hesitation the latter answered—

"I know, indeed, what the Bravo desired of me last night, but whether that was all or not I cannot say. He boldly asked me if I had the courage to enter into a conspiracy for the overturning of the government."

"But did he tell thee nothing?" asked Niccoli, who seemed strangely interested, now that matters were coming to a point.

"He told me, that if I had the courage to stand boldly forth and take up the cause for rebellion which the wrongs of my father gave me, I should find a host of friends at my back."

"Aha, then the plot is ripening. Oho, my noble lords, the eye of Niccoli is upon you. I know ye all, as though I saw your names upon a scroll. Only the Bravo—your too-ready tool—can thwart the Argus eyes of the Ten."

Thus spoke Niccoli to himself, and then turning to Alberte, he continued—

"You see, already, that some good has resulted from your arrest, for 'tis from such littles as I have learned from thee that I make up much of what I know. Why the Bravo took thee from the power of Trivisano I can well see, now that you have told me the rest. In the first place, he thought your wrongs would make you a ready tool, and he also thought that in your person would live the memory of wrongs which to this day the people of Venice have never forgiven. When the Council of Ten banished the lord Marcello from the state, they took from the people one of their firmest friends; and had he then, or within a year from his banishment, come back and raised the standard of rebellion within Venice, I verily believe he might have marched through the senate to the ducal chair, for the people loved him."

"Aye, and he loved Venice," added Alberte, with a beaming eye and trembling lip.

"That may have been," returned Niccoli; "but still you must see that in you we have

one whose influence is to be feared, if you bend towards rebellion, and your apparent intimacy with the Bravo gave us ample occasion for such a suspicion. Even now I fear that you would rebel should opportunity offer."

"Not against Venice," replied Alberte.

"Not even to gain the power thy father lost?" said Niccoli, in meaning accents.

"Not for the ducal diadem itself. I wish, indeed, that my rightful inheritance might be restored to me, and I have even thought of trying to gain it; but if I walk not honorably to it, with the free consent of the government, then I shall go to the grave without it. Yes, my place of burial will bear but the simple name of Lioni. Would to God that, ere I die, I might wrest from the grave of the council's denunciation the noble name of my father, for even with that I could be content."

"Perhaps you speak the truth," replied the spy; "but at any rate you will not be condemned without just and sufficient evidence. You would not have been so near the torture, had I known what was going on, but luckily I arrived in season. Your letter you can write at once, and after that you will find plenty here to occupy your time."

"But tell me, before you go," urged Alberte, "how long am I to be kept here?"

"As long as the council see fit."

"But I have committed no offence, and you have already gained all the intelligence I have to communicate."

"Still you cannot leave this place," said the spy.

"One thing tell me—shall I be sent to a worse place?"

"You ask more than I can tell," replied the spy; and then taking a few steps towards the door, he turned and gazed for several moments in silence upon the youth. There was a peculiar look in his eyes, and a strange trembling upon his features.

"Alberte Lioni," he at length said, "when you go from this place you may go to your death; and perhaps your steps from hither may lead you to the goal you seek—the name, the estates, the lordship of your father."

The youth sprang from his position, but the strange man was gone, and the grating of bolts and bars recalled him from the fascination of those meaning, mystic words—

"Your steps from hither may lead you to the goal you seek—the name, the estates, the lordship of your father!"

CHAPTER XV.

The palace of mourning—Isidora Vivaldi catches a gleam of sunlight, even through the darkness—The villain's visit—The fearful cypher of the Ten—The attempted abduction, and the rescue—The reptile and the lion.

ON the second day after the death of the lord Francis Vivaldi, a deputation from the senate, together with all the councillors of the state, attended at the unfortunate nobleman's palace. His two associate state inquisitors, the lords Alfonso and Blenzi, took possession of all the papers pertaining to his office, and the whole of his vast estates was taken in charge by the great council for the space of one year; all the revenues, meanwhile, to be at the disposal of the daughter, and at the end of that time she was to be put in full and responsible possession.

There is no need that we should describe, or rather attempt to describe, the grief of Isidora Vivaldi, for hers was a heart that showed not all the sorrow that dwelt within it. Angels must have wept answers to her tears, and the great heart of humanity could not but thrill to its very core with sympathy at the relation of anguish such as she felt. Throughout that vast gorgeous palace, from its dome to its foundation, hung the sable drapery of mourning, and whichever way she turned her eyes, the very walls seemed to tell her that her father was dead—that she was an orphan! Even the streets echoed with the sad notes of wailing, and upon the busy canal sounded the voice of terror and amazement at the blow which had come upon Venice. People walked the streets in silence, or in small knots conversed together upon the topic of Vivaldi's mysterious death. The same hand that had taken his life was to take more, and each senator, as he went forth from his dwelling, knew not that he should ever return to that dwelling again; when he laid down at night, he knew not that he should rise from his bed to behold another sun. Consternation, like a cloud of darkness, hung over the city.

Isidora Vivaldi was like the young yew within a mighty forest, which had alone been stricken, while the flash of the lightning and the roar of its thunderbolt still played awfully above. For a long time after the visitors had left the palace, she sat within the private study of her father, and gazed in silence upon the worn manuscripts which he had so often handled. While thus she sat, one of the servants informed her that a gentleman had just left a letter for her, at the same time handing her a neatly folded but unsealed package. As soon as she was alone, she slipped off the silken cord, and as the handwriting struck her eyes, her heart gave a quick throb from its dull inaction, beating once more in her bosom, as she read the following:—

"DEAREST ISIDORA,

"Fain would this heart send forth its last breath of life, could it thus restore to you the all that you have lost; but alas! how deeply have we both tasted of sorrow's bitter cup—how darkly rolls the tide of affliction o'er our path. That father, upon whom you rested, as the budding rose upon its parent stem, has been torn from thee; he whose heart was all goodness, and who had so kindly lighted the bright lamp of hope in my bosom, has gone, I fear, for ever. Even while I write this, I am a prisoner within the grasp of the powerful Ten; but oh! thou blessed angel of love and gentleness, even within these walls I feel the presence of thine affection in those companions of art which thou didst so kindly send to me, and you know this heart swells with gratitude in return. One joy at least is mine: for thou, loved one, believest that I am innocent of even a thought of crime. I know you do—in your heart, at least, I know that my image is reflected without the taint which suspicion has cast upon me. That I am the victim of a foul conspiracy there is no doubt. When I left the palace of your father in my gondola, I was seized by Carolus Trivisano, and confined within the damp dungeons beneath his father's palace; and after I was thus cruelly incarcerated, he taunted me in my misery by bidding me seek the rights of my father, and the hand of the lady Isidora. Cannot you, dearest girl, translate this language!"

* * * * * * *

[Here followed a clear account of all that had since befallen him, together with the infamous falsehoods of Trivisano and his son.]

"And now, fond one, let our leading star be hope. I feel that a crisis is coming; perhaps—ah! that cruel, doubtful word—perhaps I may be engulfed within the storm; but as I write to you now, a bright-winged angel seems floating above me, and ever and anon he points his silvery finger onward. Of one thing I am assured, if I go out from here a free man, I shall bear the name of my patrician father, and his mantle will fall upon my shoulders. Then you shall have a protector, if your heart will still trust to the lasting affection of   ALBERTE.

"P.S. Write to me, Isidora—write."

Again and again did Isidora Vivaldi read that note. The tears which had so long been dried in their fountain by the intensity of grief, now burst in a flood, and her heart felt lighter. Oh, she did love the imprisoned youth with a fervor which nought could shake, and in her soul she knew him innocent of crime. But the hope which Alberte had painted looked not so brightly to her. Why should it? There was a terrible reality, which spoke from the dark drapery around her, that hung like a pall over all hope.

Again the servant interrupted her meditation. A gentleman had called to see her; and brushing away the still wet tears from her cheek, she descended to the hall. As she entered the apartment, where sat the visitor, a sensation of terror crept over her, and she recoiled as though she had seen a serpent. It was Carolus Trivisano who had desired her presence.

"Ah, fair lady!" exclaimed the young noble, with a feint of deep melancholy in his manner, " allow me to be among the first of those who come to extend their greetings of sympathy in this, your time of mourning. I should have come ere this, but I would not intrude upon the outpourings of so sensitive a heart as yours!"

As young Trivisano said this, he raised his handkerchief to his eyes, and extended his hand. He would fain have wept, could those eyes have shed a tear; but sympathy had no fountain there, so his hard cheek remained dry. Isidora could not play the hypocrite; her heart was not schooled to those arts of dissimulation which are necessary to the hiding of the true feelings of nature, and instinctively she drew back her hand as she would from an asp.

"I will not refuse your sympathy, sir," she said, while the color revisited her cheek, "and I sincerely hope your tongue belies not your heart; but I cannot take your hand."

"How?" exclaimed the young noble, as he dropped the handkerchief from his eyes, which were now far from being tear-wet, "not take my hand! In what have I offended thee?"

"In that thou art a villain!" returned Isidora, forgetting all else save the utter contempt she held for the hypocritical wretch who stood before her.

For a moment Trivisano hesitated in his reply. He had determined to play the hypocrite throughout, but his resolution almost failed, as this cutting reply fell upon his ears,

However, he conquered his anger for a time, and in a tone of the most consummate duplicity he said—

"You are pleased to be facetious, lady; and still methinks thou hast chosen a strange time for such pleasantry."

"Pleasantry, sir?"

"Yes, lady; for surely you do not mean what you have said? I came hither to offer you protection, and—"

"Protection!" repeated Isidora, as her eyes actually flashed fire. "Do you talk of protection? So did the wolf once promise protection to the lamb! No, sir, I want none of it. At this moment I should feel grateful for your absence. I trust you understand me?"

"Yes, lady, I do understand you," replied the young noble between his clenched teeth; "but when I came hither with a power to protect you, I came also with another power. Aha! my pretty tyrant, within this bosom there beats a heart which can revenge as well as love—which can punish as well as protect. If you will accept my oft-proffered love, you shall be shielded from all harm; but if you refuse me again, you shall be my prisoner."

"Your prisoner!" iterated the proud girl, while the muscles of her face and neck swelled with the power that was awakened within her. "Who dares to make a prisoner of Isidora Vivaldi?"

"I dare!" returned Trivisano, with a bitter, scornful laugh, which seemed like the mockery of hell. "I came not here to be brow-beaten, nor came I here to abuse thee; but I did come armed with a power to resent insult, and to make thee a prisoner. By the command of my father, I shall take thee."

"And dost thou think thus to daunt me? thou creeping image of man—thou abortive semblance of humanity! Even though you took me a hundred times, there be powers in Venice that would release me."

"See here!" slowly and meaningly pronounced Trivisano, as he threw open his silken vest.

Isidora started back in affright. There, upon his breast, she saw the fearful cypher of the mighty TEN! Either one of these powers, alone, she would not have feared, though she might have been startled; but, take them both together—the wicked and tyrannical hypocrite, and the authority of the Ten to aid him in his evil designs—and there was much to be feared. The secret visit of one of the officers of the Ten is at any time an object of apprehension, but when that visit comes in the midst of a public state of tumultuous excitement, there is everything to be dreaded.

"Now what thinks the lady of my power?" asked Trivisano, as he witnessed with a demoniacal satisfaction the effects of his revelation.

"I think," replied Isidora, as she struggled up from the terror of the moment, "that your power is useless in your present position, for the Ten have given you no authority over innocent and defenceless females."

"That you are defenceless, fair lady, is the result of your own choice; but that you are innocent, remains yet to be seen."

"How, sir?" exclaimed Isidora, in indignant surprise. "Do you dare to insinuate that you even suspect me guil—" She did not finish the sentence, for there was something so bold and daring, and so self-confident, in the manner and bearing of the man before her, that her heart fluttered and almost sank within her.

Carolus Trivisano watched with an eagle eye the various expressions upon the countenance of the lady, and as he saw her tremble and turn pale, a quick flush of triumph passed over his features. With a look that might well have become the folded snake, he said—

"You yet have an alternative. If you will but accede to my oft-expressed wishes, and freely give me your hand in marriage, all may yet be well. Once more I give you your choice."

"Marry thee!" returned Isidora, with an expression of the most ineffable scorn, and to whom the recurrence of this foul proposition had given new life. "I would sooner submit to all the racks in Christendom, for they can touch but the body; while with thee my soul would be doomed to perpetual loathing. No, no; you cannot—you dare not—you have not the cause for the prosecution of your threat."

"We shall now see, proud lady," returned the young noble, between his clenched teeth. "You have held conference with Marco Martelino."

"Me!"

"Aye, lady; you."

"No, sir; I never saw him to know him."

"But he has visited you within this very house."

"'Tis false; oh, basely false! Once he saved my life, but I saw him not. I know not his features."

"You need not deny it, for I have evidence. At all events, you are my prisoner, and from this moment I take possession of you."

"And whither will you convey me?" asked Isidora, rather in a tone of half-suppressed defiance than in one of inquiry.

"You will attend me to my father's palace."

"To thy father's palace!" repeated Isidora, as she took a step towards the door.

In a moment more her hand would have been upon the bell-rope, but Trivisano sprang quickly forward and seized her by the arm.

"No, no, lady, we have no need of visitors. I have at hand as many as I shall need, in case of emergency."

As he spoke, he drew Isidora towards the small door which opened upon the canal, but the moment she found the villain was in earnest, she screamed for help.

"Unhand me, sir!" she cried, as she struggled fiercely, "or the servants will be aroused."

"Ha, ha! the servants are safe, and so wilt thou be, ere long. Against the power of the officers of the Ten you will find no defender."

"But she will, though!" shouted a voice from the other side of the room.

Carolus Trivisano sprang at the sound, and laid his hand upon the hilt of his dagger. He did not draw it, though, for the object that met his gaze unnerved the arm.

"Marco Martelino!" uttered the astounded noble.

"Will defend the daughter, though he may have stricken down the father," added the Bravo, as he advanced towards the spot. "Get thee hence, Carolus Trivisano, as soon as thy coward legs will carry thee."

"What! thou mean-born bravo—thou paltry hireling—thou cutter of throats—dost threaten me?"

For a moment the giant form of Martelino trembled, but in the next it changed to a dark smile, as he said—

"I told thy father—"

"Hush! for God's sake, speak not more!" exclaimed the villain, as he turned ashy pale.

"Then get thee hence at once; and dare but to set thy foot within this palace again, and thy craven neck shall no longer connect thy head and body! Dost understand me, sir?"

Like a whipped cur did the young lord turn from that apartment; but ere he went, he swore that Isidora should yet be his, and that upon the Bravo he would be revenged.

Did Isidora Vivaldi breathe more freely after the young lord Trivisano had gone? Perhaps she did; but as she turned her eyes towards the Bravo, she felt as though she had exchanged the venomous reptile for the forest monarch. She shrank from the former with a fearful loathing, while in the presence of the latter she trembled with awe-struck fear.

For some time Martelino gazed in silence upon the trembling girl, and once or twice some word dwelt upon his lips, but it remained unuttered, and in silence he strode from the apartment.

CHAPTER XVI.

The lord Blenzi upon the Rialto—His medita-
tions, and his novel interruption—The monk
and his promise—The assurance—The closed
chamber—A fearful discovery—A strange lamp
—A metamorphosis.

THE Council of Ten had been in session with the two remaining state inquisitors, Alfonso and Blenzi. It was near midnight when they closed their meeting, but yet little had been done towards the object for which they came together. The spy had given all the information concerning the Bravo which he had obtained, and he had also assured the council that he would be at the bottom of the whole mystery ere a week had passed away—a promise, by the bye, which the Ten thought easier made than fulfilled. They knew not, however, the thousand wheels which their spy had constantly in operation, nor did they begin to surmise how much he already knew, which, for the present, he had chosen to keep to himself.

The lord Blenzi stepped out from the ducal palace, after he had closed his business with the Ten, and in a thoughtful mood he took his way homeward. The moon had not yet risen, but here and there, where the light, fleecy clouds opened upon the blue ether beyond, peeped forth the twinkling stars, and as the lord passed on, he caught their images from the still canal, and for a moment he stopped upon the Rialto to gaze upon the scene. Around him lay the city of his nativity and of his pride.

"Ah," murmured he, to himself, "sleep on, dear Venice—and well mayest thou sleep. Thou art all unconscious of the worm which gnaws at thy breast; and even to thy very bosom mayest thou press the viper which shall sting thee even unto death. Would that I might read the fearful secrets which lie hidden in the womb of time, and which must have their birth in stern realities, for well I know that there be secrets there which bode some woe to thee. Sleep on, fair city, sleep; nor wake till iron-heeled rebellion starts thee from thy dreams of peace. Why hangs this load about my heart? Why these fantasies within my brain? Surely no ill can come to me, for wrong I've done to no man. Neither had Vivaldi! Ah, there's murder rife in Venice!"

"You speak truly, sir!"

Blenzi laid his hand upon his dagger, and turned quickly round; but he saw only the form of an old, decrepit monk, whose long beard contrasted strangely in its silvery whiteness with the dark cowl that covered his head.

"Whom seekest thou?" asked the noble, as he bowed respectfully to the aged father.

"I was on my way to the ducal palace, my son, but thy meditations, which thou gavest so freely to the winds, arrested me. Ah, too truly didst thou speak; there is murder rife in Venice. There hangs a blow over the poor city, which, unless it be arrested, will fall most heavily upon it, and alas! for those against whom its venom is most surely aimed."

"You speak as one who knows," said the old noble, feeling a powerful interest in the words and manner of his strange companion.

"I know but what others may know," replied the monk. "Even now I am on my way, old and feeble as I am with the weight of time, to speak what I know, and to gain the means of imparting more. Ah, sir! whoever you be, you cannot feel more for Venice than do I."

"But whom do you seek?"

"Canst tell me if the Ten are yet in session!" asked the monk, without seeming to notice the question of the other.

"They have but just risen from their deliberations," replied Blenzi.

"Then I must needs turn my weary steps back, for I sought one whom I supposed would be there."

"But whom did you seek?"

"Ah, perhaps thou canst direct me," said the monk. "I seek the lord Blenzi; he who was second in power to the ill-fated Vivaldi."

"Then you need look no further. Blenzi stands before you."

"Speak you truly?" asked the old father, in a doubtful tone. "Thou knowest that there be those in Venice whom to trust is dangerous, and I would not that an enemy should hear the secret."

"Look, then, for thyself," said the old noble, as he withdrew the mask from his face.

"Now I know thee," exclaimed the monk, "and thou shalt have my business. Over beyond San Paolo, within the house of one Filippo, a worthy citizen, there lays at point of death a man, whose heart, till now, has been all steeped in blood. But since grim death has beckoned him to follow, his soul has relented from its sinful purpose of wicked deeds, and he fain would tell us of a plot which evil men have aimed against Venice.

TRIVISANO AND THE GONDOLIER.

To the lord Blenzi alone will he communicate what he knows."

"Now," said the noble, who felt a strong inclination to follow without further question, but who still had doubts, "what assurance can you give me, that I may trust thee?"

"This," returned the monk, as he drew back his dark robe and exposed his left breast.

"And what is it?"

"Look nearer."

Blenzi looked as directed, and within one of the folds, but almost hidden by the overlapping cloth, he could just distinguish, by the light of a lamp which burned near them, the mystic cypher of the Ten.

"Go on," said he to the monk, "and I will follow thee."

"I'm glad you've thus agreed," said the old father, in his quaint and half-poetical manner, "and may God, in the fulness of his grace, feel pleased to grant that Venice shall be a gainer by your mood. The man must live till we arrive, for life was not so dim but that the taper promised some full hours yet to come. Verily, I know not what he knows; and even though I shewed him my authority for the receiving of such revelations as do concern the state, still no word would he speak to me of what he had to tell, but said the old lord Blenzi must first hear it."

"But know you not who he is, or from whence he came?" asked the noble.

"No, my son. All I know is, what he has been, not what he is at present; all I know is, where he is, not where he may have been."

The walk was not long; and though the noble kept his hand upon the hilt of his dagger, still he could detect nothing in the manner of the old monk to make him fear that he should have occasion for its use; and it was with a comparatively confident step that he entered the dwelling which the monk had pointed out as that of the citizen Filippo.

"Now where does this man lay?" asked Blenzi, as he stood within the hall.

"This way, my son," replied the monk, as he took a taper which still burned upon the table before him, and opened a door leading up a stairway.

For a moment the noble hesitated;—he did not fear the monk, but he knew not what dangers might lie beyond. But then the cypher! Surely, no man in Venice would dare to wear that dread symbol without the knowledge of the Ten, and, surely, the Ten would never have given that mystic cypher to a man who might not be trusted. Still the old inquisitor held himself upon his guard, and as he followed the monk up the stairway,

his sharp dagger was loosened and half drawn from its sheath.

"Within that room, upon the bed, you'll find the man of whom I spoke," said the monk, as he opened a small door at the head of the stairway.

The room contained nothing but the bed and a few chairs, and without hesitation Blenzi entered; but hardly had he stepped within, when the door was closed. He sought the bed, but it was empty! He looked around, but no one was there save himself! A lamp burned upon the side-board, and by its dim light, which sent forth a sickly, yellowish hue over the place, he sought the door, but he found it firmly locked upon the outside; then he went to the windows, but he could only see the dark wall of the building opposite. Blenzi would have cried for help, but when he opened his mouth his lungs refused their duty. In the excitement of the moment he had not noticed the subtle power that was gaining the ascendancy over him; he had not noticed that his legs were weakening beneath him, or if he had, he thought it the result of his agitation; but now he realized the horrors of his situation.

Weaker and weaker grew his limbs, and quickly and more quick came the heavings of his chest, while his mind began to waver upon its throne, and his brain to reel. He instinctively sought the bed, and without the power to even murmur his thoughts, he fell upon its surface. He felt no pain, nor did he experience any anguish; a soft, gentle hand seemed pressing upon his heart, as though to quell its beatings, and a strange feeling of expiring ecstacy thrilled through his veins. His eyes, half shut in by the drooping lids, rested upon the lamp. That yellowish flame, which now flickered like a star beyond the misty cloud, seemed to grow in size, till it swelled a huge ball of fire, to the very ceiling, its yellow grew to gold, then blue, then red, until at length it took the rainbow for its semblance; and while yet the noble gazed upon its thrice-enchanting power, his dull eyes trembled in their sockets, then stood a moment still, then closed in utter darkness. The lamp seemed conscious that no one gazed upon it now, for with a slight death-struggle it shot forth its last dim, flickering column, and then it died!

In a few moments the bolts were drawn aside, and the monk cautiously peered into the room, and finding that all was still and dark, he drew the shade from a lantern which he carried in his hand, and softly entered. He approached the bed, and laid his hand upon the noble's heart. When he found that the work was done, he threw back the dark cowl from his face, let the long white beard drop to the floor, drew up almost erect his doubled form, and Marco Martelino now stood over the prostrate form of the lord Blenzi!

"Ah, Blenzi," he murmured, as he turned and took the small lamp from the table, "you knew not that the poor flame which lit thee to thy bed was the silent, subtle thief that stole away thy life! You knew not that each flicker of the blaze was but a summons for thine own heart's weakening. Certainly, 'twere a blessing to die by so sweet and gentle an agency. That same power which took Vivaldi in his sleep, has, in another form, put thee to thine. Ah, Venice, now you may tremble again, for the Bravo will most surely be revenged!"

CHAPTER XVII.

The meeting in disguise—The unexpected entrance —The pledge renewed—The result of the intelligence of Blenzi's death—The Ten, and the startling disclosures which were made by the spy.

NEAR one of the docks which was situated below the arsenal, stood an old, dilapidated dwelling of light greyish stone. On the same night, and at the same time, when Blenzi was wending his way to the fatal chamber of the Bravo, an old sailor, clad in the rough habiliments of his vocation, came up from a boat which had just landed at the dock, and entered the old building. Ere long, another and another, dressed in the same style, followed up from the water, and knocked at the door for admittance. He who had at first entered hesitated for a moment, and demanded the word.

"The Commonwealth," returned the foremost of the two, and in a moment more they were admitted.

In less than half an hour ten men had collected within that old house. The doors were all secured, and a lamp was lighted, but as its dim rays fell upon the forms around, not one of those who were there could tell who was his neighbor, so complete were the disguises which they wore. At length, one stepped out from the rest, and with the open palm of his left hand upon the top of his head, he waved the right thrice in a circular motion, and as it stopped, the index finger was pointing towards Heaven. The others all bowed a token of recognition, and then each passed singly by him, whispering in his ear, as he did so, the words, "*Imperium in imperio.*"

"All is right," said he who seemed the leader, and dropping the mask from his face, the lamp shone upon the features of Marino Trivisano.

The others followed the example. There were the lords Carolus Trivisano, Castello, Dolfino, Polani, Masto, Cordino, Florado, Mentoni, and Steffani.

"My lords," said Trivisano, "have you watched well how hung the suspicions of the Ten with regard to the troubles in Venice?"

All gave an answer in the affirmative, and the old noble continued—

"Does there rest in your minds a single reason for believing that aught of suspicion yet falls upon any of us?"

All answered, "No."

"Then," said Trivisano, "I am at a loss to comprehend the meaning of Martelino's conduct. The youth Lioni I had reason to fear, and so I had him safely confined; but the Bravo has seen fit to release him, and, as you all know, he is now in the hands of the Ten; but it seems they have been enabled to gain no information from him. Before the tread of Martelino again is allowed among us, I would have your opinions respecting him. Shall we trust him further, or shall we take the only means in our power of silencing him for ever?"

"Perhaps he will explain that for himself, and save your lordships further trouble," pronounced a deep voice; and in a moment more the object of their doubts emerged from the darkness in the extremity of the apartment. As Martelino approached the conclave, he gazed for a moment on the astounded nobles, and then continued—

"The lord Blenzi sleeps a sleep that knows no dreams. Even but now I left the place where rests his cold body. Thus far have I gone in your service, and if you now cease to have confidence in me, I will trouble me no further. I did take your prisoner, Trivisano, and I hoped to have bent him to my wishes; but when that failed, I left him for Niccoli, as the chased hunter drops a piece of meat to arrest the progress of the famished wolf. In this I've done no harm to your cause, but rather a benefit, though in truth I did thwart your designs, Trivisano; but for that I've no extenuating word to offer. Does Carolus

Trivisano wish for explanation further, on points particularly concerning him?"

The young noble thus alluded to turned pale for a moment, but quickly regaining his self-possession, he replied—

"No, sir; if there be aught between us that needs an explanation, I shall seek it in a more fitting place."

The Bravo smiled at the youth's threatening manner, and then turning to the rest, he said—

"You've heard some explanation, and you probably remember my oath: that I would not give one word or action that would implicate you in the least, till I first found that one or more of you had harmed or betrayed me."

"No; 'twas not an oath," interposed Castello.

"Well, then, let it be an oath," returned the Bravo, "for here, by all the powers of Heaven I swear it. But, my masters," and here he spoke fearfully distinct and slow, "dwelt there no thought of harm to me in the words I but just now heard from the lips of Trivisano?"

"It was no thought of harm," quickly returned the old noble, slightly trembling as he spoke, "but 'twas only the discussion of thy conduct, which you have but now so satisfactorily explained. Were I, or Castello, or any of the rest to be suspected of treachery, we should expect the others to speak their thoughts freely upon it. We fear not to trust thee, so thou mayest rest assured on that point. But tell us, for we have a right to know, how you gained admission to this building?"

"I came through a passage known only to myself," returned the Bravo, "and, for my own safety I must for the present keep that a secret."

They seemed satisfied to let the Bravo retain his secret, and at once proceeded with their business. Ample arrangements had thus far been made, and a full account was given in of how all matters stood. When the meeting broke up that night, Marino Trivisano had in his possession the names of twenty-one nobles, and over three hundred citizens, who had bound themselves to sustain the leaders of the plot.

The next morning dawned upon Venice, and as the bright sun came shining upon her domes and flashing windows, the news began to spread that the lord Blenzi was missing. Every ear had heard it, and every tongue had repeated it, and all, too, whispered, in connection with this fearful fact, the name of Martelino. But ere the king of day had been

two hours from his eastern starting point, all doubts were put at rest, for at every street-corner, and upon every lamp-post, appeared the following placard:—

"A REWARD OF 10,000 PISTOLES *Will be paid to the person who shall bring, dead or alive, MARCO MARTELINO to the Ducal Palace. Venice mourns the death of two of her noblest sons, VIVALDI and BLENZI, who have been foully murdered by him. Said Martelino is now within the city, nor can he escape therefrom; and should any person, knowing where he is, and not feeling able to capture him, give such information to the undersigned as will lead to his arrest, he shall receive the whole of the above-mentioned reward. (Signed)*   NICCOLI."

To the above was also affixed the seal and signature of Francesco Dandolo, the Doge, together with a thorough description of the Bravo's person.

People everywhere were struck with consternation. Every stranger was watched, and even avoided, as though he had been an evil spirit, while business seemed for the time suspended. More than two hundred persons had been taken from the docks and canals, and hastened before the council, but the Bravo still eluded them all. A large, stout-built man, who might have a slight roundness of the shoulders, could not be half an hour in the streets without being seized upon and hurried away; in short, no one seemed to know his neighbor, so intently were all eyes seeking for the dread form of the Bravo. The Council of Ten was in session, but they had little to say. From the thoughtful, troubled face of the chief spy, their eye turned towards the now empty chair, where, but the night before, had sat the unfortunate state inquisitor. A case such as the present they had never been called upon to consider, and they seemed to feel the same undefinable dread which was working among the people without. Some of the Ten were upon the commission which tried the lords Tiepelo, Basseggi, and Querini, during the reign of Gradenigo, and they all remembered the fearful results of that fatal day on which Venice had wept so much for her best blood. But even that dark and terrible plot created not half so much alarm as the mere shadows of the present cast before it.

The lord Alfonso sat there alone in his office. He was now the most powerful man in the commonwealth, and yet he was at the same time the weakest, for fear bowed him down. Upon his shoulders now rested a power superior to that of all the citizens, and even the Doge himself. Even the Council of Ten held no control over him, for he stood in the same relation to that as that did to the senate—he was independent of their power—and yet at the very thought of the fearful Martelino he turned pale, and trembled within the chair of his office.

"Niccoli," said the chief of the Ten, "is there not the slightest news of this man? Have you not yet got any clue to him?"

"Only this, sir," replied the spy; "I have obtained intelligence of some of his disguises, and thus I am in hopes to secure him; but he seems to have a different one for every day in the year."

"But if what I have heard is correct," returned the chief, "there is one thing which he cannot hide, and that is his Herculean frame."

"But he can so disguise it, nevertheless, that it cannot be identified," replied Niccoli. "Once I saw a monk, not over seven and a half spans high, but he looked full nine around the waist—that man was Martelino."

"But you did not know it then?"

"No. The next day he whispered in my ear, as I stood upon the steps of St. Mark, and told me of it."

"Told thee of it?"

"Even so. But when I turned, I saw only an old lady, who asked me if I knew who that dark man was that spoke in my ear, and when I asked her where he was, she replied that he had mixed with the crowd."

"And you saw him not again?"

"Yes, I was conversing with him then."

"How? Conversing with Martelino?"

"That old woman was he."

"But how did you know it?"

"That very night I sailed with him upon the canal, and thought the while that I was with an old white-headed gondolier, who for half a century has pulled his boat for the accommodation of the patricians. When I landed, he very graciously informed me that the old lady with whom I had spoken was the Bravo. I disbelieved him, but as his gondola shoved off from the shore, he pulled off the old man's beard and hair, and the moon shone full upon the dark features of Marco Martelino."

"But did you not give him chase?" asked the astonished chief.

"I might as well have chased a moonbeam. Twenty gondolas were after him, but the very wall of the canal seemed to swallow him."

"Then, how can you ever take him?" asked

old Alfonso, who had listened with a trembling interest to this strange recital.

"There are some peculiarities, my lord," replied Niccoli, "which may not be hidden, and 'tis by studying these that I am to succeed. Of one thing I am assured; if we do entrap him, we shall find him far different from what you expect. Marco Martelino is not what he seems; of that you may yet be satisfied."

"But that he is a murderer, and that most foul, we already know. What else seems he?"

"He seems the hireling cut-throat, the common killer; but I am confident there is some deep, dark secret hidden in his bosom, which none save himself on earth doth know. I have studied his character, and I have traced his actions; and though he is an enemy to be feared, still he is not one to be despised. Venice hath at some time done him some foul wrong, and for that he will be revenged."

"But his revenge must not go on," exclaimed the excited chief. "If his progress can be arrested in no other way, the council shall pardon him all past offences: aye, even though the act be so grievous, still it must be done. The blood of Vivaldi and Blenzi calls for vengeance, but the lives of the rest bid us pause and reflect."

"Let it not be so yet," said Niccoli. "Ere another falls, I will strain my every nerve. I know that Alfonso is singled out for the next victim; but he must not leave the ducal palace, at least till I have made another effort."

"Ah! I thought so," murmured the aged man, while a tear coursed its way down his time-worn cheek; "but why, oh why, should the fiend of murder seek out me?"

"Listen," exclaimed the spy, while his eyes flashed around upon the council. "Can ye not read the scroll? Can ye not decipher the mystic language of these dire disasters? Why is it that the government is thus crippled at its head? The next blow, if it comes, will be upon the Savi; and this, too, for the same purpose—that Venice, when attacked, may fall more easily a prey to rebellion."

The members of the council made no answer to this, but gazed in silence upon the working features of their spy. As he stood there regarding them with a fixed and determined look, they thought they could read in that face a confidence in himself which told all his tongue could have uttered. Upon Niccoli they rested all their hopes.

CHAPTER XVIII.

The creation of the young artist—The visit of the
spy and Alfonso, and the effects of the picture
upon the latter—The disclosure—Innocent, but
still a prisoner—Remarkable change in the
effects of the painting upon the painter.

EVEN though Alberte Lioni was a
prisoner, still time hung not heavily
on his hands, for the companions of
his dear profession were all around him, and
in the soul-absorbing occupation he lost all
thought of time. To be sure, there were
clouds above and about him, but, for all that,
he could command at pleasure one gleam of
sunlight at least. Then another gleam than
that of art had shone in upon the seclusion of
his prison—a gleam than which earth could
have sent him none more bright. It was a
letter from Isidora Vivaldi. She had said
nothing of Carolus Trivisano, nor of the
Bravo, for she feared that the relation might
occasion more uneasiness than there was any
occasion for. With this kind letter next his
bosom, the youth had placed the last touches
upon a picture which had grown up under
his hand; and, as we look in upon him now,
he stands gazing in rapture upon the creation
of his art. But ere long the admiration of
art gave way to another feeling, and while he
gazed the warm tears began to tremble upon
his eyelids and trickle down his cheeks.

Upon the canvass, which yet rested on the
easel, looked forth a humble cot, half-hidden
by shrubs and trees, in front of which were
two figures. One was that of a middle-aged
man, the other a fair-haired youth. The latter
had a light hat upon his head, while across
his back was slung a small travelling pack.
His features the youthful artist had not dared
to paint, but had covered the face with the
left hand, through the fingers of which several
tear-drops were starting. It wanted no
physiognomy, however, to enable the beholder
to read the soul of that boyish traveller; for
in the form, position, and in those tears, and,
above all, in the bearing of the remainder of
the picture, it could all be seen. The other
figure stood erect; the build was powerful,
and the aspect commanding. With one hand
he grasped the extended right hand of the
boy, and with the other he pointed towards
Heaven; the head was uncovered, save by the
dark hair which floated in the breeze, and the
eyes, slightly upturned, streamed with tears.

Oh, it would take no deep student of art

to read a picture like that. The stricken
father—the departing son—the heaven-called
blessing, and the soul-stirring farewell. Then,
too, there was nobility in that father's face—
a nobility of the soul—of humanity, as well
as of birth. In fact, the man who had studied
a dozen pictures in his life would not have
failed to read, in that artist's creation, the
banished noble.

While Alberte stood gazing upon his picture, the door of his prison was opened, and
the spy, accompanied by the old state inquisitor, entered the apartment. For several
moments the lord Alfonso stood with his eyes
fastened upon the canvass, and then, while a
deep melancholy rested upon his features, he
murmured—

"Ah, Marcello, what magician's power has
thus called thee from the tomb?"

"And do you recognize him?" quickly asked
Alberte, partly in surprise at the old noble's
manner, and partly in pride that his efforts
had resulted so well.

"A hard fate was thine, thou most unfortunate man," continued the inquisitor, not
seeming to notice the question of the young
artist. "Oh, Venice, when thou didst put
forth Giovanni Marcello from thy councils,
thou lost one who might have made thee
better and wiser."

As these words fell upon the ears of Alberte
Lioni, he started as he would had the glad
trump of an angel sounded in his ears, and
laying his hand tremblingly upon the old
noble's arm, he said—

"Did you speak of him whose face and
form you see upon my canvass?"

"Yes," returned Alfonso, still gazing upon
the picture.

"And do you believe that Giovanni Marcello was innocent? Do you believe that he
was true and faithful to Venice?" asked the
youth, almost fearing to hear the answer, lest
his suddenly raised hopes should be as suddenly crushed.

"Innocent, asked you?" returned Alfonso,
for the first time turning his eyes upon Alberte.

"Yes, my lord—do you believe that my
father was innocent?"

"I know he was!" returned the old inquisitor.

"Tell me, sir—oh tell me, can you prove
this?" almost shrieked the youth, as he pressed
his nervous fingers so tightly around the old
man's arm as to make him flinch.

"Yes, good youth, the proof will ere long be made in public, and 'twas to give thee this assurance that I accompanied Niccoli hither."

"Oh, I thank God for this!" ejaculated the youth, as he withdrew his hold upon Alfonso's arm, and raised his clasped hands to Heaven. "Look down, oh, my father, and hear this avowal, for once more in the land of thy birth thy name shall be honored and thy memory beloved." Then turning to Niccoli, he exclaimed—

"Thou, too, Niccoli, knowest this to be true."

"Yes; I have long known it."

"And did not tell me!"

"That was because I would not raise a hope in the bosom of one who might himself immediately crush it."

"What mean you by that?"

"You know why you were brought here?" returned the spy.

"I know on what suspicion."

"Well, I thought it a pity that you should have a name and title but for the purpose of again sinking it in shame."

"Oh, how false—how horrible was that suspicion," murmured Alberte, while a cold shudder crept over his frame at the very thought; and then, as a new idea seemed to flash upon his mind, he said, while his lip quivered and his eye burned with the fire of an earnest expectation—

"Then you must know that I, too, am innocent of the charge you would have brought against me. Say, is it not so?"

"You have spoken the truth," returned the spy.

"Then I may leave this place."

"Nay, good youth—not yet."

"Not leave it?" exclaimed Alberte, in surprise. "Why should I be kept here longer?"

"Because it is necessary," laconically answered Niccoli.

"Do the Ten so decree?"

"No. I will that it should be so."

The young man looked up into the face of the spy with wonder and astonishment. There was no sign of sternness, but, on the contrary, the features of Niccoli wore a kind and benignant expression; and recalling a murmur of displeasure which he would have uttered, the youth asked—

"May I not at least know for what I am still held a prisoner?"

"Not at present," returned the spy; "but when you do know, you will see that no blame can attach to the authority which holds you."

"But you can at least tell me how long I am to remain here."

"Yes," answered Niccoli; "you will remain here three days yet."

"And then shall I be at liberty?"

"Yes."

"And you, my good lord Alfonso, will prove to the great council what you have told here to me," continued Alberte, turning to the old man.

"It shall be proved, young man, whether I do it or not," returned Alfonso; "and now I trust that your remaining stay here will be lightened by the knowledge that when you go hence, you will take your station among the noblest of Venice."

"I thank you, sir—from my soul I thank you," returned Alberte, "for your kindness in thus lightening my load of doubt and anxiety."

Again old Alfonso gazed upon the picture which Alberte had painted, and murmuring some inaudible sentence to himself, he took the arm of the spy, and together they left the room.

After they had gone, Alberte Lioni walked slowly and thoughtfully up and down the place of his confinement. A thousand thoughts and feelings came rushing through his mind, but two only found a resting-place in his busy brain. The one was the memory of the father whose name he could even now see upon the temple of honor; the other, that fair being, in whose pure, unsullied bosom dwelt that love which was to bless and make him happy here on earth. While these thoughts were stretching away into the future, the youth stopped in front of the picture. The first raptures of the artist's soul had passed away, and now he looked upon it with the eye of a connoisseur.

What strange feeling is it that makes the painter's face turn so deadly pale? What is it that makes him tremble so, as he gazes upon the silent canvass? His father's face looks not as it did. Around the brow, the eyes, the nose, the mouth, and even in that black waving hair, there seemed to have come a strange and unaccountable alteration; Again and again he strained his eyes upon those painted features, but still they wore the same fearful change.

At length a towering form rose up to his mind's eye—a dark, forbidding, and an evil form—which lowered upon him from that canvass like a giant of misfortune. Turn it which way he would, let the light strike upon the canvass as it might, still the same change clung to it. In vain was it that the painter examined each feature by itself—in vain that he studied each line and lineament; yet, when taken as a whole—when he gazed full upon the face which but a few moments before had filled his soul with rapture—he was struck with a fearful, undefinable dread. The muscles of his face changed their tension like an ill-tuned harp, the fingers were clenched in agony, and his knees tottered like reeds beneath him.

Alberte Lioni sank back into a chair, and buried his face in his hands.

"Oh, what vision is this that thus oppresses my brain?" murmured the youth to himself. "No, no, it cannot be—tis a mere phantom of an excited imagination; and yet how it speaks from that canvass—how every line of my brush has helped to build up the very image I would exorcise. Alas! and must all my new-born hopes be thus crushed at once? Must I be thus doomed—No, no?—away, for thou liest, base, deceiving picture!"

It was a long time ere the youth rose from that chair; but when he did so, that evil phantom still haunted him.

CHAPTER XIX.

The meeting upon the landing—The concerted plan of villany—The gondolier and his sister—Isidora and her maid—The startling cry upon the canal—The deception—A kind heart made the cause of cruel disaster.

THE night was dark, but not stormy; the moon wanted some hours yet before her face would look upon the city; and the stars were all shut out by a thick haze, which enveloped the streets and canals in a mantle of almost impenetrable gloom. It wanted some minutes of ten, when Carolus Trivisano stepped forth from his father's palazzo, deeply disguised, and made his way towards the canal, where he walked up and down by the landing-stairs for several minutes.

"Does the stranger go by water?" asked a gondolier, as he respectfully doffed his hat to the young noble.

"Why do you uncover your head to me?" asked Trivisano.

"That I might see thee better, and, perhaps, serve thee better."

"That's right. Modetti has seen you, then?"

"Yes. He told me to-night how I was to receive you."

"Your name is Barbo, then?"

"Pietro Barbo, sir."

"Did Modetti tell what I wanted of you?"

"He did not know, sir."

"You are right. Step to the right here, a little farther from the stairs—there. Now, do you want to fill your purse?"

"I know of nothing at this moment that would please me better," replied Barbo; and even through the darkness the quick flash of satisfaction could be seen, as it illumined his dark features.

"What say you to ten golden pistoles?"

"Tell me how I may make them," returned the gondolier, as his hand sought the hilt of his poniard, in token of his readiness to do anything for such a sum.

"You will have no use for your steel."

"So much the better."

"Do you know the dwelling of Seigneur Francis Vivaldi?"

"Yes."

"Do you know the lady Isidora?"

"Yes."

"I would have her in my power."

"But that is a difficult job," said the gondolier, in a thoughtful mood.

"Not if you have the wit which Modetti told me you had," replied Trivisano.

"But how am I to take the lady from her chamber, while the place is full of servants?"

"I expect, of course, that you will use stratagem, and that you must study up for yourself."

Pietro Barbo thought for several moments, and at length he said—

"If you will pay me ten pistoles on the spot, and five more when the job is completed, I will do the thing this night."

"Pay you beforehand?" exclaimed Trivisano. "I know not yet that I can trust you."

"Why may not you trust me as well as I trust you? It strikes me that the stealer of defenceless females ought not to boast."

Trivisano's hand was upon his dagger.

"Oh, don't touch that, my lord."

"My lord?" repeated the young noble, in surprise. "Why do you lord me?"

"Oh," replied the other, with a light chuckle, "there's no use in denying it. A common citizen wouldn't have touched his dagger so quickly. But in this business we are equals—unless, indeed, you choose to use your weapon, and in that case you might find a superior."

Trivisano saw at once the position in which he stood; and relaxing a little of his *hauteur,* he said—

"Never mind that at present. If you will bring Isidora Vivaldi to this spot by midnight, and deliver her safely into my hands, the sum you name shall be yours."

THE ABDUCTION OF ISIDORA.

"Agreed!" replied the gondolier.

Carolus Trivisano placed ten pieces of gold into the hand of Barbo, and after admonishing him to be cautious in his proceedings, he turned once more towards his home.

Pietro Barbo jingled the gold in his hand, and then depositing it in his bosom, he hastened away towards one of the casinos which stood near the western wing of the church of San Paolo. Here he inquired for his sister; and ere many minutes a pretty courtezan, some eighteen years of age, came tripping to the door.

"How now, you lazy dog," was the first remark of the girl, as she saw her brother; "you are after more money, I'll warrant."

"Not so, Stella," replied Barbo, as he drew her out at the door beneath the piazza. "Listen!"

"Ah!—gold?"

"Yes, sister, all gold; and I am yet to have five pieces more, which shall all be yours, if you will help me to earn them."

"And how can I help you?"

"All I want you to do will require but a little effort—not above a mere fainting fit or so.'

"Oh, San Marco! I would rather do anything else, Pietro, than to faint. No, no, I can't do that."

"Not in earnest, Stella—only a sham, that's all. You see there is a young patrician who has taken a notion to fall in love with a proud girl, and she don't seem to appreciate him; so he has hired me to take her away from her home, and place her in his hands. Now, will you help me to do it?"

"If you will use no violence, yes."

"Oh, I promise you that; and it is to avoid violence that I want you."

To the mind of Stella Barbo, there was no harm in an intrigue of this sort; and one who has the least acquaintance with the state of Venetian society at that time, and even as late as the latter part of the eighteenth century, will not wonder at it. Those peculiar virtues which cast the highest charm upon the social relations of a people were almost totally disregarded, and fortunate was that female who could bud into an honest womanhood beneath the atmosphere of Venice.

It was with a light and buoyant step that Stella threw her light mantle over her head and shoulders, and followed her brother, and as she groped her way along the dark street, guided only by the sound of his leading footsteps, no thought ever entered her mind that she was about to aid in crushing the heart of a poor defenceless orphan. Alas! Stella knew not what mines of wealth may lay in a human heart, and she knew not that a heart could be broken, for across her own there had never come aught but a passing cloud. Love was to her like a butterfly—it had no beauty but when 'twas on the wing.

Isidora Vivaldi was in the small drawing-room attached to her own chamber, and by her side, upon a seat lower than her own, sat one of her maids. Near them a tall balconied window opened upon the canal, and just as we notice them now, the latter was opening the sash.

"Still dark and dreary, is it not, Celia?" asked Isidora, as the girl looked out upon the water.

"Yes; I can hardly see the canal. Oh, it's a terrible night!"

"Not quite so terrible, Celia, as when we were last upon the water."

"No, no, in truth it is not," replied the girl with a shudder. "That was a horrible night, and but for the young gentleman we should not have been here now. Oh, if I was a lady, I should love that youth!"

A slight smile passed over the face of Isidora at this honest remark; but 'twas a mere gleam of the moment, for on the next the deep gloom settled back, and the tears started to her eyes.

"Don't weep, senora," urged Celia, as she left the window and sat down at her lady's feet. "They will not surely harm him—they certainly can't find it in their hearts to use him wrongfully."

"You know not why I weep, girl," replied Isidora, as she gazed with much affection into the face of her kind-hearted maid. "You know not half the sorrow that weighs me down."

"Alas! that so good and kind a mistress should have cause to be so unhappy. I used to weep when my father died, for he was a good father, even though he was poor. I was too young to weep when my mother died; but when your good mother died, I cried and felt sad, because she was almost a mother to me. But oh! how happy your poor mother must be now, when your dear good father has gone to meet her. Perhaps they'll change into angels some time, and come down to bless you. I love to think, when I am alone, that my father lives in Heaven; and it makes me happy to think that I never do anything to make him miserable."

Isidora gazed upon the calm features of Celia, as she uttered her passing thoughts, and simple as was the picture, it had much influence over her. There was so much resignation, so much true piety, and so much kindly feeling, that she could not help bending forward and resting her head upon the girl's shoulder.

"Look out again, Celia," said Isidora, as she raised her head, "and see if the moon is yet up."

Just as the girl reached the balcony, there came up from the canal a loud piercing shriek, and with a startled expression Cecilia turned to her mistress, and exclaimed—

"Did you hear that?"

"Yes, Celia," replied Isidora, as she sprang towards the window. "Did you see where it came from?"

"I saw a splash in the water just below our stairs. That was a woman's voice most certainly."

"Hand me my mantle, Celia, and you run down immediately, and get some of the servants with torches. It may be our turn now to lend assistance."

Celia sprang to obey her mistress, and Isidora drew the mantle over her head, and hastened down to the water. When she reached the landing-stairs, she found her worst fears realized, for just below her she could plainly distinguish a stout man in the act of drawing a female from the water.

"Help, help, for Heaven's sake!" exclaimed the boatman, as the light of a torch gleamed over the canal, "the poor lady has fainted!"

"Here, my good man, pull your gondola up to the stairs, and we will take care of her." said Isidora, as she bade one of the servants go down with a torch.

The boat was soon at the landing; and three of the servants immediately stepped down and took the senseless form of the lady up the stairs.

"Is the lady Isidora Vivaldi here?" asked the gondolier, as soon as the servants reached the head of the steps.

"That is my name," answered Isidora, who was just upon the point of following the unfortunate sufferer.

"Perhaps she would like to know who the lady is that has just been carried up?"

The servants were all busily enaged in their attentions to the fainting girl, and those who could render no assistance were pressing forward to get a glimpse at her features, so that their mistress was wholly unobserved by them. Isidora harbored not the least suspicion of anything like danger to herself, and without hesitation she turned back. Quick as thought Pietro Barbo pressed a thick scarf against her mouth with the right hand, and winding his left arm at the same time around her waist, he lifted her into his boat. It was but the work of a moment to bind the scarf tightly around her head, and with a quick push he sent the boat far out into the canal, holding on upon Isidora with one hand, while he sculled with the other.

As soon as he was out of sight from the torches of Vivaldi's palace, Pietro let go of the oar, and taking a small strong cord from the locker, he firmly bound Isidora's arms behind her. She could not speak, nor could she utter a sound—nor did her captor open his mouth to make any explanation; but as soon as she was secured, he seated himself upon the rowing-thwart, and, with both oars in their beckets, he swiftly forced his gondola through the dark water, towards the place where we last saw him with Trivisano.

"Ah, Barbo, you are a prince of gondoliers," exclaimed Trivisano, as he caught a glimpse of the female form in the stern of the boat. "Did you get her away without creating any alarm?"

"She never uttered a syllable, sir," replied Barbo, "and there she is, safe and sound."

The young noble paid the remainder of the stipulated sum, and in a few moments Isidora was placed in his own gondola, and quickly rowed away. She had heard the voice of Carolus Trivisano, and she knew that she was in his power. Alas! there was no one now to aid her, nor could she make her misery known; and with one deep groan of anguish, she sank into the oblivion of utter unconsciousness.

CHAPTER XX.

Modetti and his work—The spy in the scent—The forged keys—The secret passage—Some important documents change owners—Carolus Trivisano is interrupted in his meditations—The emissaries and their prisoner.

IT was an hour after Carolus Trivisano received from the hands of Pietro Barbo the prize of his night's excursion, that Pascal Modetti sat alone in the small secluded chamber in the upper part of the lord Marino Trivisano's palace, where the reader saw him at the opening of our story. A small lamp burned upon the bench before him, while by its light he was examining a small curiously-constructed key, from which he had just taken a keen file. From a shelf before him he took a plaster pattern, which he adjusted with much precision, and then placed the key within it, where it turned with the utmost ease and nicety; and as he drew it forth a smile of satisfaction passed over his features. From the same shelf on which had laid the pattern of plaster, he then took five more keys of about the same size of that which he had just finished; and having thoroughly examined them, and passed them carefully through their respective patterns, he laid them aside, and broke the patterns in pieces. Not long after this job was finished, a secret door on one side of the room was carefully opened, and the Spy of the Ten entered; he looked around the apartment with cautious eyes, and then approaching the workman, he said—

"Well, Modetti, are you ready for me?"

"Yes, Niccoli; the keys are all ready. I put the finish upon the last one just before you entered."

"And are you sure they will fit?"

"Yes; for I got the impressions most perfectly, and the keys fit exactly. They move like dies."

"Then Venice may owe thee her thanks, Modetti; for these small bits of metal will give to me what our city has long needed, though she knew it not. Ah, Pascal, thy master's house would not so long have remained in quiet, had our councillors but have known the secrets which these results of thy midnight labors will disclose."

"And how have you so long known this?" asked Pascal, as he gazed upon the spy with a look of admiring astonishment. "How have you so long had a knowledge of that which the lord Trivisano holds so secret?"

"That is one of the many things which even the Ten do not know. Aye, they know not even that such secrets exist, and for the present you must be satisfied with knowing a little more than do the Ten."

"Well," replied Modetti, "I have no desire to know that which should be kept secret. But here are the keys, and you may be assured that they will answer your purpose."

Niccoli took the keys and turned them over, one by one, in his hand; and after he had thoroughly inspected them, he placed them in his pocket, remarking, as he did so—

"You've made good work of it, Pascal, very good; and if they prove as effective as the others which you have made me, I shall be more than satisfied."

"You need but to try them, Niccoli, and I will wager my place in your confidence that they will not disappoint you."

"No, no; do not wager that, Pascal, for you shall, ere long, find that your place in my confidence is your greatest inheritance. I have

proved you in every respect, and you are just the man which Venice needs."

"I thank you for your kind opinion," replied Modetti, "and I like it the better, because it has ever been my greatest aim to merit it. But now that you have got the keys, there is another thing which I would tell, unless you have other business first."

"There is none so pressing that I may not stop to hear what you have to tell."

"You know that Francis Vivaldi left an only daughter."

"Yes; the lady Isidora."

"Last night—for I think it is morning now—Carolus Trivisano came to me, and asked me if he might trust me with a secret message. Of course I told him 'yes'; and having gained his confidence, he explained to me his business. He wanted me to find a gondolier with whom he could trust an expedition of the utmost importance: one who was quick-witted, but at the same time indifferent to the work he was engaged in, so long as he got the pay for it. I told him I knew just the man he wanted, one who would cut a throat for five golden pistoles; and I referred him to Pietro Barbo."

"Good," ejaculated the spy, as he heard this name of one of his most trusty emissaries.

"Well," continued Modetti, "he also wanted me to find out this Barbo, and make some arrangements for a meeting, and also to concert a signal by which he could recognize the man without fear of detection. This I did, having previously instructed Pietro to let me know as soon as possible the result of his expedition."

"And has he told you?" asked Niccoli, who seemed much interested in the relation.

"Yes. He came as soon as he could after the business was settled."

"And what was it? How was the lady Isidora concerned?"

"That's it, sir. She was the very object of the whole plan. My young noble wanted to get possession of the lady; and he has done it. But it is better as it is, than it might otherwise have been; for now we know the whole transaction, the lady is comparatively safe."

"Do you know where the lady is?" asked the spy, while he trembled with excitement.

"I know that she is in the palace, sir, somewhere; but I know not exactly in what room."

"Of course the villain will not trouble her to-night."

"No," replied Modetti; "for he, I know, is now in his own chamber. I have watched him narrowly since he came in."

"Watched him yourself?"

"No. There are others in the building who obey my wishes. Ah! I have a pretty thorough knowledge of all that transpires around me, thanks to your instruction."

"Where is the young man's chamber?"

"Do you know where the old man's cabinet is?"

"Yes."

"And you know the long corridor at the head of the stairs which leads up to the right of the cabinet?"

"Yes."

"Well, his chamber is the second room on the left after you ascend the stairs."

"That will do," said Niccoli; "and now let me have the lantern."

Modetti drew forth a small drawer from beneath his bench, from which he drew a pocket lantern, and having trimmed and lighted the lamp, he handed it to the spy.

Niccoli left the room by the same way he had entered, which led him into a circuitous kind of corridor that ran around the building, between the inner and outer walls, which connected, by means of secret slides, with all the important rooms in the palace. It was of course very narrow; and in most parts only wide enough to allow a goodly-sized man to pass. Through this passage the spy took his way; and after traversing some distance, he descended a winding flight of stone steps, which led him to the second story of the building. He had not gone far, after reaching the foot of the steps, ere he stopped; and holding the lantern close to the wall, he commenced a minute examination of the masonry. At length he found the object of his search, which was a square stone, in one respect differing from its neighbors, with the exception of a small cypher, which seemed to have been indented with a chisel near the top. This stone was carefully eased from its position by swinging on two perpendicular gudgeons, revealing, as it did so, the wooden panelling of the room beyond; and after listening a moment, Niccoli moved a tiny slide, which was curiously constructed in the mortice of the wood, and which opened a small aperture, not much larger than a pin's head, through which he peeped into the room.

The spy may have felt slightly disappointed, as he thus took a survey of the apartment, for he not only beheld Carolus Trivisano, but the father was also there; however, he quickly placed the slide once more over the hole, noiselessly shut back the stone, and then hastened away, saying to himself as he did so—

"Never mind, young man, I shall attend to you, ere morning, and in the meantime, instead of listening to a conversation between two traitors, which could in no way make me

wiser, I will finish my night's business with your father."

Niccoli hurried on, and in a few minutes he stopped before a stone similar to that which he had just closed, but bearing a different cypher, which he opened; and having slid back the panel beyond, he entered the private cabinet of the lord Trivisano. Without other hesitation than merely to assure himself that all was safe, he took the forged keys from his pocket and commenced searching the secret compartments of a large case which seemed to have been erected with the original building. In the first compartment which he opened, he found several rolls of parchment, but after having thoroughly examined them he replaced them just as he had found them; but in the second he met with something of more importance, for after casting his eyes over the pages which he took from thence, he rolled them up with a smile of satisfaction and placed them in his bosom. Another and another locker was opened; from each of which he selected such documents as he thought proper, and at length, as he opened the fifth, his eyes fell upon a somewhat time-worn parchment, which he grasped with an eager hand.

"Ah!" murmured he to himself, as his eyes sparkled, "I cannot see, Trivisano, why you should have taken this precaution to hide such matters as these. Methinks the flame would have been their best hiding-place; but you have run your own course, and now the secrets of your own bosom shall rise up like gaunt spectres of the past to condemn thee. Your fate is sealed, my lord Trivisano; but even pity, that slightest of all earthly tributes, will never be linked with thy memory, after thou art dead and gone."

Niccoli felt a sensation of sadness creep over his heart as he closed the last compartment of the case; and with a noiseless step he left the cabinet. The panel was closed, the stone swung back to its place, and once more he turned his steps to the apartment of the young Trivisano.

This time, as he placed his eye to the small aperture, he found that the young man was alone, pacing up and down his room in a slow and thoughtful mood. Niccoli waited till his back was turned, and then quickly pushing back the panel, he sprang into the room; the slide instantly closing behind him, and as Carolus turned in his walk he found himself confronted by the man whom he had the most reason to dread on earth. For a moment Trivisano stood aghast; then collecting himself for a desperate game, he asked—

"To what am I indebted for this visit, sir?"

"I come for information from one who

wears the cypher of the Ten," replied Niccoli, in a sarcastic tone, as he bent his eyes like two stars upon him.

"And what do you seek?"

"The lady Isidora Vivaldi is missing."

"Well, and what have I to do with that?" returned Trivisano, vainly endeavoring to assume a careless look.

"Merely to answer my question," replied the spy, still keeping his gaze fixed upon the young noble.

"And if I know nothing of it, what then?"

"I have not come here, sir, to ask you concerning subjects of which you are ignorant, nor have I come here to trifle. Last night you had the lady Isidora forcibly abducted from her home, even while the weeds of mourning were still darkening above her brow, and you conveyed her to this place in your own gondola. Now I would have you conduct me to her."

"Who told thee that base lie?" exclaimed Trivisano, while he trembled with mixed feelings of rage and fear.

"It is no lie, young man. Now, take your choice, either conduct me to the lady, and that, too, quickly, or else I will conduct thee to the Inquisition."

"Conduct *me* to the Inquisition?" repeated the young noble. "You dare not to do it, sir. It takes another hand than thine to arrest a noble of Venice."

"But not to arrest one of the deepest-dyed villains in Venice," added Niccoli, as he began to tremble with the indignation that was creeping over him.

"Do you dare—"

"Hold, sir," interrupted the spy in a thundering tone. "I dare do anything that pleases me. Now, do my bidding, and mark ye," he added, as he stepped nearer to the villain, and bent upon him a look of so fearful meaning that words were almost unnecessary, "if you make the least show of resistance—if you even dare to look resistance—I'll crush thee as I would a stinging viper, and before the council I'll answer for the act."

Carolus Trivisano gazed for a moment into the face of the spy, and then, with a quick movement, he drew his dagger from his belt and sprang forward; but the intended victim had his eyes too keenly fixed to be taken by surprise, and stepping on one side he seized the uplifted arm as he would have seized a feather, and wrenching away the dagger, he struck the villain a blow upon the side of the head, that felled him senseless to the floor. He stopped not to notice how severe had been the effects of the blow; but taking the key from the inside of the lock, he passed out and secured the door after him, and then hastened down into the lower hall, from which he stepped out into the street. As soon as he reached the pavement, he took from his pocket a small silver tube, which he placed to his lips. A shrill, trembling sound reverberated through the street, and ere long it was answered by the appearance of two men—one a gondolier, and the other a cobbler, whose stall was upon the Rialto.

"This way," said Niccoli, as he turned back towards the hall; "I have work for thee here."

The two emissaries of the Ten, who had been called to the assistance of the chief spy, followed their leader without asking any questions; and in some five minutes the lord Carolus Trivisano was on his way, in their keeping, towards the dungeons beneath the ducal palace.

CHAPTER XXI.

Marino Trivisano spends his last night within his palace—His interview with the spy, and its results—A soul of purity led to the Divine—A startling announcement—The dawning of a new epoch.

THE lord Marino Trivisano, after he had left the apartment of his son, sought his own chamber, where he immediately sat down to a small table and commenced writing. He had lost the fervor of his former days, and the hand of time had set marks upon his brow; but other marks there were upon that brow than those of age—marks which the corroding iron of an evil soul had set there, as indelibly as does the lightning shaft sink its track into the stricken oak. His hand did not slide over the pages before him, as was its wont, but it went tremblingly about the work to which its scheming mind had put it.

Oh, what a pity it is, old man, that thy last days should be spent in evil; that, while the dark angel of death is even hovering over thy head, thou shouldst be plotting wickedness against thy fellows, for as sure as you sit now by your table, this is the last day that will

ever close upon your liberty. The next shall
see thee within the power of that government
against which you have so long been plotting;
and may the Lord, in his infinite grace, have
mercy on your soul, for to the TEN that is
an attribute with which they have nothing
to do.

"No, no," muttered the old noble to himself, as he pushed the paper from him, "I cannot write to-night. Night, did I say? No,
for yon moon tells me it must be morning,
and still I have not slept, nor shall I sleep
again till I am on a throne! Ah, there's
magic in that word—even now I see a sceptre
within this hand. I wish I were a little surer
of my plans—I wish I knew what keeps the
Ten in such constant sittings; for, by San
Marco, they cannot spend thus much upon
the Bravo. But then my friends are good
and true; and as for Martelino, he dare not
be otherwise, for his own head sits too lightly
on his shoulders; so away all thoughts of
danger, for ere another moon rises upon Venice,
she shall be relieved from the yoke that now
binds her down, and she shall take her place
among the kingdoms. Aye! she shall have a
king, and one, too, who shall not be the mere
plaything of councils and savi."

While Trivisano was musing thus to himself, he was startled by a rap at his door, and
hastily hiding the half-written sheet which lay
upon his table, he arose and turned the key;
and when he opened the door, he gave entrance
to the chief spy.

"You are up late, my lord," said Niccoli, as
he gazed upon the troubled countenance of
the old noble.

"Not later than yourself, sir," returned
Trivisano.

"That's true; but then I've had business.
I am now on an errand of importance."

"And to me?" said the noble, while a slight
shade of alarm passed over his features.

"I suppose I must do it with you. I wish
for the person of the lady Isidora Vivaldi."

"Isidora Vivaldi!" repeated the old man,
as though her name surprised him.

"Yes, my lord, the lady is in your palace;
and, furthermore, she was forced here."

"Then you must seek my son; for if the
lady is here, as you say, it is his business, and
none of mine."

"Your son, sir," replied Niccoli, while he
gave a meaning-look into the old noble's face,
"is ere this within the dungeons of the ducal
palace."

"How? within the dungeons!" exclaimed
Trivisano, starting with fear and alarm.

"Yes; I have taken him away not fifteen
minutes since."

There was no indignation—no resentment
nor anger in the feelings of Marino Trivisano
at that moment, for fear alone found a place
there. The first thought that flashed across
his mind was of his plot—of its detection—
and for several moments he silently trembled
in the spy's presence.

"You seem deeply affected at the intelligence," remarked Niccoli, as he noticed the
effects of his communication upon the old
man's mind.

"Of what has my son been guilty? What
has he done?" asked the father, as he once
more found his tongue.

"What has he done? He has broken the
peace of the city, and trampled her laws under
foot."

"How?—how?" gasped the terror-stricken
man, as the fear of detection thickened in his
soul.

"He has hired the ruffian of the canal to
steal away the daughter of Vivaldi, and with
her arms pinioned, and her cries of mercy
stopped, he forced her to this place. I tell
thee, Trivisano, that Venice will not brook
such insult to the sacred honor of her orphan
homes."

"Is that all?"

"It is all; and methinks it is enough."

Marino Trivisano drew a long breath, and
once more his heart beat easier in his bosom.
The fearful cloud had passed, and his secret,
he thought, was safe; and turning a bold look
upon the spy, he said—

"You take much liberty, sir, at all events,
in thus entering a nobleman's house; but if
the rash boy has been guilty of such misde-
meanor, he should certainly be punished. If
you will follow me, I will search for the lady
you seek."

The old noble led the way, and as he did
so, his face, which was turned from the spy,
wore an expression of malignant triumph. He
thought that the power which now upheld the
powerful Niccoli would soon be no more—
that he himself would have the handling of
those whom he now feared.

"In that room," said Trivisano, as he stopped
before a door in one extremity of the palace,
"you will find the lady Isidora, and of course
you are at liberty to do as you please with her."

Niccoli thanked the old man for his kindness, and withdrawing the bolts, he opened
the door, and entered the small drawing-room
which led to the principal chamber beyond.
Here he stopped at the inner door and knocked,
and receiving a request to enter, he at once
obeyed it.

Isidora Vivaldi had risen from her seat, for
she dared not trust herself upon the bed; but

as her eyes rested upon the form of the spy, the trembling which had seized her frame was stilled in a moment, and with all the confidence of a child towards its parent, she sprang forward, and laid her hand upon his sinewy arm.

"Oh, sir," she cried, as she raised her eyes imploringly to his face, "you have come to save me—I know you have."

"Yes, lady, I have come to save thee; and he who has thus dared to trample upon your rights will have power to trouble, thee no more. I trust that I am in time to save you from all harm."

"I have not been troubled, sir, since I was brought hither, excepting by my own fears, but even they were enough to harrow up my soul."

"Has the young noble ever offered violence to you before?" asked Niccoli.

"Yes, sir. Once he even came to my dwelling himself and attempted to take me away; but at that time I was rescued by the man whose very name makes me shudder, and causes my blood to run cold."

"Was it the Bravo?"

"Yes," answered Isidora, with a shudder.

For a moment the fair girl gazed into the face of the spy after she answered, and then, as the simple pronunciation of that fearful name brought to her mind more vividly the picture of her dreary orphanage, she burst into tears.

"Why should you weep thus, lady?" asked Niccoli, as he drew her towards the open window, where the cool air might blow upon her brow.

"Why should I not weep?" she answered, as she pushed back her dark tresses, that the breeze might play more freely around her heated temples. "What has fate not done for my misery?"

"Fate, did you say?" repeated the spy, as he fixed his piercing eyes upon her. "Did fate give that life to the old man whose loss you mourn?"

Isidora understood the reproof, and for several moments she was silent; but at length she raised her head, and said—

"I know, sir, that he whose heart is free from the anguish which loads down mine can see with a clearer vision the inconsistency of the mourner's repinings; but grief like mine makes the soul its upper servant, and from its life-springs naught comes forth save bitter, burning thoughts of sufferings."

"Come hither," said the spy; and drawing Isidora still nearer to the window, he continued, as he pointed to the bright full moon, which had not long been up from its bed in the Adriatic—

"Look upon yon bright orb, which now sends its cheering light upon Venice. But a few hours since all was darkness and gloom, and a damp thick cloud enveloped the city. The same Power which laid that cloud over us has now taken it away. He has sent his night-queen to illumine the dreary places of his earth, and all around us, in the blue arch of his heavens, He has set those sparkling gems which seem to syllable their Maker's praise. Ere long, even they shall melt away before the mighty majesty of his greater light, and Venice shall bask in the bright effulgence of full-dawned day. Now tell me, lady, will not that Power which thus overlooks a mere planet, that may at some future time be crumbled into atoms, care still more for an immortal soul—a soul which throughout the endless ages of his eternal reign, shall revolve within the halo of an endless peace—a peace made glorious by the very fact, that from within its influence not a human soul which He has made shall be shut out for ever?"

Isidora still wept as her strange companion spoke, but her tears were not so bitter, though they flowed full as fast as before.

"I cannot but feel thankful for a friend like thee, for thou speakest to me as one who has a heart to feel that which he utters. And yet," she continued, as she brushed away the tears from her cheeks, and gazed with a peculiar look of mingled confidence and reproof up into his face, "you did but a few days since paint to me fears which were as dark as night itself."

"Because I would have prepared thee for the blow which I feared was to follow; but, lady, I knew not that thy father was to die."

"Alas! the blow has come, and it has stricken my every joy; but I will not repine, for well I know that my Creator doth his pleasure, and in my holy, happy faith, I believe that what is his pleasure is my highest good. Yet my tears shall flow; nor would I stop them if I could, for my blessed Saviour wept when his friend was taken away, and by his Divine example, tears have been made as heavenly dews which fall with a cooling influence upon the fever of our griefs."

Niccoli looked with astonishment upon the almost angelic features of the beautiful girl, and his own heart beat in answer to her sentiments. For some minutes both stood by that open window, and gazed out upon the moonlit scene; but even the most casual observer would have known that their thoughts were not following in the direction of their gaze, for there was a calm tranquil expression upon their features, which accorded not with the

ALBERTE AND ISIDORA.

brilliant and varying scene that lay stretched out around them.

"Come, lady," said the spy, as he at length stepped back from the window. "It wants but a short hour of daybreak, and I would have thee seek thy rest as soon as may be. I will conduct thee to thy home, but to-night your presence will be needed at the ducal palace."

"At the ducal palace?" repeated Isidora, in surprise.

"Yes."

"But for what am I wanted?"

"You may be wanted to give your evidence against a criminal."

"Stop, sir—stop!" exclaimed the fair girl, as she withdrew herself from the hand that would have supported her, and fixed a determined look upon him. "Do you speak of Alberte Lioni?"

"No, lady. Alberte Lioni will to-night go free, and he shall bear the name of Lioni no longer."

"Then who else can it be?" uttered Isidora, rather to herself than to her companion.

"Marco Martelino."

"The Bravo?"

"Yes."

"And has he been taken!"

"Not yet," returned the spy; "but within my possession I have papers which inform me where he will be to-night. Ah! Martelino, your tread in the senate chamber will be short, for the Spy of the Ten has you now within his power, and if this good arm withers not from my will, Venice shall fear you no more. But come, lady, throw your mantle over your shoulders, and follow me; and mind, now, not a word of what I have told thee must thou lisp to a living soul."

As Isidora Vivaldi left the palace of the lord Trivisano, she felt that a new epoch was about to dawn upon her; but whether its dawning should be for weal or for woe, still lay hidden within that dark future which even hope itself failed to penetrate.

CHAPTER XXII.

A chapter in which our story has a conclusion, and in which all our characters are disposed of to the entire satisfaction of the author, and, he humbly trusts, to the satisfaction of his readers.

THE sun has again risen upon Venice, and again has it gone to rest in its western home; the people have once more sent forth their merry song and happy greeting; once more closed their occupations for the day; and once again are they sporting upon the hundred canals, seeming unconscious of everything save the sports and pastimes, the joys and pleasures, or the pains and misery of the present. Towards the ducal palace the senators and the members of the council were beginning to wend their way, and as they went, either upon the pavement or upon the canal, they wore upon their countenances those sure indications of wonder which manifest themselves when men are unexpectedly called upon for the transaction of an important business of the nature of which they are ignorant. Some there were who knew the nature of the call, but they were very few, and to all questions they gave merely a significant nod.

The large hall of the senate was open only at the main entrance, and only the usual guard was stationed there. When the lord Trivisano entered, he looked nervously around, but everything wore its usual aspect. The officers of the chamber were in an easy social chat; the soldiers at the door seemed conscious of nothing more than a common duty, and with a comparatively easy step he ascended to his seat. At length the lord Castello entered, and the moment his eye caught the form of Trivisano he stepped quickly forward to where the old noble sat.

"Speak not in a manner too earnest," whispered Castello, "but let us appear to smile at our light thoughts. The signals are ready—one is upon the piazza without, under charge of a faithful man; one at the house-top of the next corner; and one at St. Mark; and the men are all placed ready to obey them at the moment."

"But have you seen the Bravo?"

"Be not too earnest, or we shall be observed," whispered Castello, with a light merry laugh. "I have just left the Bravo upon the piazza of St. Mark. He wears the disguise of the Genoese ambassador, and his entrance into the hall at ten o'clock will be the signal. Everything without is secure, and we have only to make sure of our game in the hall. I am sorry that the lord Alfonso has escaped; but that cursed Niccoli smelt the fire, and he has kept the old inquisitor safely confined. But never mind, there is consternation enough already for our purpose. The rest will come dropping in at intervals, but do not recognize them; they are all right.

While Castello had been speaking, he had lolled in an easy careless manner upon the front of Trivisano's desk, and his conversation was frequently interspersed with hearty bursts of laughter, so that no one would have believed, had they even suspected its possibility, that he was plotting for murder and rebellion.

The hall was at length filled; the nobles were all in their seats, and shortly the Doge, accompanied by the lord Alfonso and two dark-robed inquisitors of the lesser court, who had been called upon to fill the chairs of Vivaldi and Blenzi, entered, and the former took the ducal chair. Hardly had the duke of the commonwealth called that vast assemblage to order, when the door of a small anteroom, nearly in the rear of his seat, was opened, and the Spy of the Ten, followed by Alberte Lioni and Isidora Vivaldi, entered the chamber. The two latter were seated near the Doge, who smiled graciously upon them as he beheld their care-worn and troubled features; but some there were who did anything but smile when they saw the young artist thus within the hall. Marino Trivisano turned uneasily in his seat, gazing first upon one and then upon another of his coadjutors, but none of them seemed to notice him; for, as they sat nearer the larger doors, a strange and unusual sound, like the clang of arms, fell upon their ears, which reached not his. A general movement took place in the hall, as those nearest the entrance betrayed the surprise which the noise occasioned, but ere many minutes the clang died away, and once more all was still. While all eyes were turned towards the Doge as if to inquire why this silence reigned, Niccoli stepped forth from the place where he had stood, and advancing towards the large open space within the centre of the hall, he was the first to break the stillness.

"Your most serene highness," he said, addressing the Doge, "and you, nobles of Venice, know full well that within the last few weeks our good city has been thrown into the utmost state of alarm by the fearful threats and still more fearful deeds of Marco Martelino. None knew why he did these things, nor how he did them, but a weeping, sorrowing people tell us they are done. Long have you looked to me as the man upon whose shoulders the duty of seeking out these things had fallen, and to the utmost of my ability have I endeavored to do your bidding, and this night I trust your enemies will be no more able to do you harm. Within my very hand I hold a paper which contains the particulars of a most daring and bloody plot which was this night to have been executed within this very chamber."

For an instant the spy stopped and gazed about the hall. Consternation and alarm were pictured upon every countenance, and each looked upon his neighbor in silent inquiry. Marino Trivisano turned white as a ghost, but the others of the conspirators grasped the hilts of their daggers and stood ready for defence. Niccoli advanced to the seat of the Doge, and handed him the paper, remarking as he did so—

"I found this, your highness, in the private apartment of the lord Andria Morosini."

The old senator, whose name had been called, sprang from his seat, and while the utter consternation of the moment deprived him of the power of utterance, he would have rushed to the chair of the duke, but Niccoli held him back. Trivisano breathed again, for he thought his false plan had served him, and his companions in guilt let go their daggers.

"Horrible! horrible!" murmured old Dandolo, as he read over the names which were signed to the paper he held in his hand; and then, while a cold shudder passed over his frame, he handed it back to Niccoli, saying, as he did so—

"You know your duty—let it be done."

The spy made a movement towards the large doors, and as they opened a strong guard of soldiers entered the hall.

"Seize upon the lord Andria Morosini, and hold him your prisoner," exclaimed the Doge, as he started up from his chair.

"Hold, your highness," returned Niccoli, as his eyes flashed with an unwonted fire. "The marshal knows his duty." Then turning to the leader of the soldiers, he continued—

"You know your prisoners—take them."

What means that movement of the marshal! The Doge was thunderstruck at what followed. There sat those nobles whom he had expected to see taken, and nine others were prisoners in the hands of the soldiers. Trivisano, Castello, Dolfini, Polani, Masto, Cordino, Floridi, Mentoni, and Steffani, all of them nobles of Venice, stood bound before him. They had been taken so suddenly, so unexpectedly, that no opportunity for defence had been given them.

"I see you are surprised, your highness," said Niccoli, as the prisoners were secured; "but you shall now have the truth. That paper which I handed to you was but a false light, a mere sham, thrown out by Marino Trivisano for the purpose of covering, in case of premature detection, his own and his accomplices' guilt. Here is the true plot!"

As he spoke, he handed to the Doge the real plan which he had taken from the cabinet of Trivisano. That grey-haired traitor knew the parchment the moment he saw it, and but for the support of his captors he would have fallen to the floor. He knew that his race was run, and without uttering a syllable he gave himself up to hopeless despondency. That giant power—AMBITION—no longer held him up; his heart no longer felt the spur of his daring hopes; and while the forms of those around began to grow dim and indistinct in his fluttering vision, he sank back upon a seat.

"Oh! may God and St. Mark defend us!" ejaculated the Doge, as he read the plan of that murderous plot. "But,"—and he trembled as he uttered it—"this fearful, terrible, Bravo—this Marco Martelino—is still at liberty! Cannot Venice be delivered from further deeds of his dreadful vengeance?"

As the Doge ceased speaking, Niccoli strode forward, and while an agitation, never before known to affect him, shook his frame, he gazed in silence around upon the assembled multitude. At length his eyes rested once more upon the old Doge, and in a calm steady tone, he said—

"My lord duke, the person of Marco Martelino is in my power, either to retain or to deliver up."

"In *thy* power!" exclaimed the Doge.

"Marco Martelino!" cried Alfonso.

"The Bravo!" came from all parts of the hall, while all seemed to look and tremble as though they expected to see the fearful object of their terror rise up from the very marble pavement of the floor.

"Yes," returned the spy, with a melancholy and downcast expression; "I can deliver up to your keeping and to your will your much-dreaded enemy; but ere I do this, there is one other matter I would have settled."

"Name it," said the excited Doge.

"To you, your highness, belongs the superior privilege of introducing matters of importance to the great council. They are to-night all present, and to your disposal I give this document."

As he spoke he drew from his bosom a parchment roll, and handed it to Dandolo. As the Doge read it over, he turned first deadly pale; then a deep flush overspread his features, and raising his eyes to the face of the spy, he said—

"This was written years ago; but by San Marco! 'twas a fearful, deadly plot. And has the lord Trivisano been so long a traitor?"

"You understand the purport of that instrument, do you not?" inquired the spy, without moving a muscle.

"Certainly," replied the Doge, with a shudder. "I see that it is the minute plan of a rebellion, full as bloody in its conception as was this from which thou hast just now saved us; and I see, too, that Marino Trivisano was its projector."

"Then here is a paper, my good lord duke," continued the spy, as he handed another roll to the Doge, "which I have taken from the archives of the Ten. Will you have the goodness to read it?"

Francesco Dandolo took the paper, which bore upon its back the closed seal of the Ten, and with careful gaze he read it through. As he closed, a strange light beamed from his eyes, and starting to his feet, he exclaimed—

"Now, by my faith, good Niccoli, I see all that thou wouldst have me," and then, while his limbs trembled with the fearful agitation that raged within, he turned to the wondering nobles and cried—

"May God give us pardon, my lords and nobles, for the foul wrong the state has done to one of its noblest sons. Within my hand I hold two papers: one of them is the true plan of a plot for the entire overthrowing of the Venetian government, drawn up by the lord and senator, Marino Trivisano, twelve years ago; the other is another plan of the same plot, and drawn at the same time, and written by the same hand, and, like the instrument which I first received to-night, bearing the forged name of an innocent man. Upon the authority of this forged instrument, aided by the evidence of the traitorous villain who wrote it, the good lord Giovanni Marcello was banished, while Marino Trivisano, the real culprit, has gone free? Speak, Trivisano, how stands this mighty guilt upon thy soul?"

At the first mention of the paper which he had thought safe within the secret recesses of his cabinet, and which he had only kept for the aid it might give him in other operations, the lord Trivisano had raised himself from his fallen position, and had heard all that the Doge had said. As the flashing eyes of the duke rested full upon him, he strained his weakening orbs to their fullest capacity, and, without rising from his seat, he replied—

"Alas! my sun has set in utter darkness, and all my hopes are gone. Venice must still continue to bear the weight of her thousand useless officers, and I—I—shall never see a CROWN! Yes, my lord duke, I *did* plot, twelve years ago, for the subversion of your tyrannical government, and Giovanni Marcello was an innocent victim of your ill-timed justice."

Until the present moment Alberte Lioni had kept his seat; but he could sit still no longer, and springing from his chair, he exclaimed, as he advanced towards the Doge—

"My lord duke, after what has been brought to light here, may I not demand of the council, through your highness, that the name and title of my father be restored to the senate? May I not demand, as the only son of Giovanni Marcello, that his estates be restored to me?"

It took the council but a few moments to render in a decision which was based upon such palpable evidence, and ere long the Doge arose in his place, and in a loud voice proclaimed—

"Senators, and nobles of Venice, the state, through ignorance, hath done grievous wrong to the lord Giovanni Marcello, and his memory hath been wrongfully held in contempt; but the guilt must rest alone upon the sin-stained soul of him who hath so foully and basely deceived us; but it yet lays in our power to somewhat repair the injury. The banished noble, alas! is no more—the weight of his country's wrong has hastened him to a distant foreign grave! But his memory shall be honored—his title shall be restored—his name shall once take its place upon the patrician roll, and his estates shall go to his son by legal entail." Then turning to the young man, who still stood before him, the old Doge continued—

"To you, young man, the great council return the name you justly inherit. You are no longer Lioni, but Alberte Marcello, a noble of Venice, and an heir to a seat in her supreme council."

The lips of the youth parted, and he would have returned an answer; but if he spoke at all, his words were drowned by the loud shout that went up from those around, and a hundred eager hands were stretched forth to grasp the newly-found noble. Alberte Marcello returned their greetings with happy tears of thankfulness, and at the first opportunity he glided through the crowd and sought the side of Isidora Vivaldi. He grasped her trembling hand within his own, and then gazing for a moment into her tearful, but yet placid countenance, he murmured the simple name—"Isidora," and laid his head upon her shoulder. For the moment that fair girl lost her own griefs in the sudden rapture of seeing him whom she so fondly loved raised to the fruition of his highest hopes; but a sense of melancholy soon pervaded her soul again with its dark beams, and though she felt happy for another, yet she felt forlorn for herself.

"Now," said the Doge, as the assembly was once more in order, "we must look to thee, Niccoli, for the fulfilment of your promise."

"And you would have the Bravo

"Yes," returned the Doge, with a perceptible tremor.

The spy stepped forward, and while a strange trembling shook his stout form, and a light tear-drop glistened on either lid, he swept that large assembly with his keen gaze, then turning to the duke, said—

"You will find Marco Martelino, but in him you will lose your Niccoli for ever!"

As he spoke, the long robe of his office fell from his shoulders—his powerful form bent slightly forward till the back turned to a gentle hump—the light wavy hair was taken away from his head, and where, but an instant before had dwelt the cunning, quickly varying gaze of the spy, now towered, in its majesty of conscious power, the dark, bold, and daring features of the dreaded Bravo!

For several minutes not a person spoke in the large hall, but every heart beat with a fearful quickness as they beheld this mysterious metamorphosis, and with trembling awe they gazed upon that strange man as they would upon an uncaged lion. Trivisano and his companions no longer wondered that the plot had been discovered, but they *did* wonder that their captor should thus condemn himself to certain death. Martelino waited till the first shock of astounding surprise had passed, and then, unclasping his belt, and laying his heavy sword, together with his sharp dagger, upon the table of the Duke, he said—

"Now look upon the man you have so long feared. Marco Martelino stands before you, and he waits your pleasure."

"Do my eyes deceive me, or is this a fearful reality?" murmured the old Doge, as he strained his eyes upon the towering form before him. "Is it possible that we have lost our preserver in the person of the bloody Bravo?"

"And is he not your preserver still?" asked Martelino, without changing a feature.

"Alas! 'tis too true," returned the Doge; "and yet he is a murderer!"

"My lords," said Martelino, as he raised his head and looked proudly around him, "I have this night saved Venice from almost sure destruction. In what have I offended, that you brand me with murder?"

"In what?" repeated the Doge, wondering at the strange assurance of the Bravo. "Where, tell me, are the lords Vivaldi and Blenzi?"

"Where?" repeated the Bravo, in turn. "Where should they be, at such a time as this, but in their seats?"

Instinctively every eye was turned to the

spot where sat the state inquisitors. These two dark-robed men had removed their cowls, and a loud cry of astonishment went up as the people beheld, instead of those whom they had thought mere substitutes, the well-known features of the two missing nobles!

Isidora Vivaldi rose to her feet and would have started forward; but her father came quickly down, and while her heart leaped and her every nerve trembled with the delirium of so sudden joy, she laid her head upon his bosom, and the thanksgiving which the tongue could not utter flowed forth in happy tears.

From the two old nobles who seemed thus almost to have risen from their graves, the eyes of the people turned to the Bravo. He saw the inquiring gaze, and he knew that utter astonishment had deprived them of the power to question, and, sweeping the dark locks back from his brow, he asked—

"Have ye aught against me now?"

A simultaneous "NO!" burst from all lips, and at length the Doge stepped down from his throne, and grasping the hand which but a moment before he had thought red with blood, he said—

"Let me, in behalf of the people of the commonwealth, grasp the hand of him who has this night saved Venice! And now," he continued, "may we not know the deep secret which lies hidden beneath your mysterious manner? May we not know why you sought revenge against Venice?"

"My lord duke," replied the Bravo, in a tone so deep and meaning, that all were startled by its strange power, "years ago Venice did me a foul wrong, and in my soul I vowed that I would be revenged. With an untiring step and a steady purpose have I followed up my determination, and to-night my revenge is consummated. Venice cast me forth from her councils; she branded me as a traitor, and she took from me my fair name; and now I have saved her from destruction in the hour when she knew not her peril."

"Revenge, did you say?" murmured the old Doge, while his eyes filled with tears. "Ah! yes, 'twas a revenge—a noble, godlike revenge! But who are you? There is yet something we do not know."

"Does no one guess the BRAVO'S SECRET?" asked the strange man, as he drew his slightly-rounded shoulders up to their natural form, and turned his flashing eyes around. "Can you guess it now?"

As he spoke, he threw off the brown shirt which he had worn, and beneath it flashed the rich velvet doublet of a Venetian count and senator. He did not change a muscle of his features, but there they were, in all the boldness and commanding power of their former cast, still towering in the majesty of nobility, and still darkened by the flowing sable locks that had marked the Bravo.

Alberte alone comprehended the truth; he now could translate the mystic language of his picture; for, with the simple word "FATHER!" upon his lips, he sprang forward, and was clasped in the embrace of GIOVANNI MARCELLO!

*   *   *   *   *

The senate chamber is once more still and quiet, for all ears are listening for an explanation from the lips of the lord Marcello.

"You wonder, my lord duke, and you, nobles of Venice, at what you have seen," commenced Marcello, "but in a few words I can explain it all. When you banished me from Venice, I knew that Marino Trivisano had given evidence against me, but I knew not how deeply he himself was guilty; but after I had obtained permission for my son to return to his native city, under another name, and pursue his studies, I received an anonymous communication informing me that one of the most powerful nobles of Venice had forged the paper upon the evidence of which I was condemned, and that the true plot was even then in existence, in the possession of him who had written the false one. My suspicions at once fell upon Trivisano, for I had heard that he was granted the use of my palace; and I immediately determined to commence a thorough search into the affair. With this intention I assumed an easy, but still impenetrable disguise; then giving out that I was dead, and taking the name of Niccoli, I came back to Venice and went to work. My operations soon arrested the attention of the Ten, and by degrees I became the chief of your civil police; and in this capacity I began to get an inkling of a desire on the part of one or two nobles to upset the government. Then it was that the idea of a new disguise occurred to me; but the few years of exposure had so darkened my complexion, and the very idea of Marcello was so distant, that when I assumed the character of the Bravo, I threw off all disguise, with the exception of a hunch in the shoulders, which served to give me a more ferocious expression. In this character I was not long in gaining a notoriety; for though I did nothing but threaten, still my threats were so dark and mysterious, and so bloody and ferocious in their conception, that the name of Marco Martelino was soon sounded from one end of the city to the other as a man who would not hesitate to cut the throat of the duke himself, if he could be paid for the job. It was not long before Marino Trivisano sought me out, and by degrees I worked myself into his confidence, and was at length made acquainted with the plan of a new conspiracy. I was hired to murder the three state inquisitors and the chief of the six superior councillors, and I knew if the work was not done I should fail to get at the bottom of their plans, so I agreed to do it.

Vivaldi was the first to be removed; and fearing to trust him with my secret till I had him within my power, I administered to him a most powerful sleeping potion, by means of inhalation, while he was in his bed, and as soon as he was completely prostrated by its power, I took him to the convent of San Marie, where, as soon as he revived, he consented to remain. Blenzi was the next; but as I knew not the secrets of his palace, I used stratagem to secure him. When he was out of the way, I found that the consternation was so great that I had not better carry the deception further; so, in the character of the spy, I contrived to keep the other two close within the ducal palace, which gave the Bravo sufficient reason for not killing them. Of course you will readily conceive how easy it was for the Bravo to elude pursuit, and also how easy it was for Niccoli to obtain his intelligence. I found, also, that Trivisano meditated evil against my son, and once, you know, he contrived to confine him in the dark dungeons beneath his palace; so, to shield him from all further danger, I made pretence of suspicion against him, that I might keep him safely in prison; but before I did this, I tried to see if there dwelt in his bosom a spark of rebellion; and even in the character of the fearful Bravo I could not repress the warm tears of paternal pride as I found him noble and true. Thus I followed up my plans, from step to step, until I not only got a full knowledge of all matters connected with the plot which has this night been brought to light, but I also sifted to the bottom the foul conspiracy by which you were once so basely deceived, and by which I was so deeply wronged. I have suffered much and long; but the happy consummation of my highest hopes, and the confidence once more of my fellow-citizens, is a sufficient remuneration for all; and if you, my lord duke, and nobles of Venice, have lost the services of THE SPY

OF THE TEN, you will at least have the satisfaction of knowing that you are in possession of what was once alone THE BRAVO'S SECRET."

For a moment after the lord Marcello took his seat, which he did by the side of his son, all was silent within that hall of state; then came forth a gentle murmur, like the premonitory rumbling of an embryo earthquake, which gradually swelled and grew in power till it arose to Heaven, the enraptured bursting of a thousand human hearts, all overflowing with thankfulness and joy.

* * * * *

Within the palazzo of Francis Vivaldi stood some of the most important personages of our story. There was the lord Marcello and his son; Vivaldi and his daughter; Blenzi and Alfonso; Francesco Dandolo, Doge of Venice, and several of the Capi. As we look in upon them now, all is hushed; and as the light from a hundred sparkling lamps sends its rays across their features, a look of expectation is plainly beaming there. The lord Giovanni Marcello embraces his son, and then leads him forth. Francis Vivaldi takes the fair Isidora by the hand, and imprinting a warm kiss upon her brow, he says—

"My dear child, in what I am about to do I feel a happiness and pride that sends the warm blood of other days once more bounding through my veins; but though I give thee to another, I cannot give up one grain of that love which, springing from the pure heart of my daughter, must ever be the source of my highest earthly joy."

As he spoke he placed her hand in that of Alberte Marcello, and ere another word was spoken, a holy father of St. Mark stepped forward and performed that sacred ceremony which united as one, for ever, those two hearts that even from prattling childhood had been interwoven by the silken cords of the soul's purest affection.

"Ah!" said old Marcello, as he wiped a tear from his dark cheek, and took the hands of the happy young couple in his own, "though God may at times send upon us clouds so black and impenetrable, that the soul sinks beneath them, yet the eye of a Christian faith may overlook them all, and see, within the care of him who doeth all things well, a bright and happy day which hath no night, and 'WHOSE JOYS AND PEACE SHALL NEVER HAVE AN END.'"

END OF THE BRAVO.

LIST OF WORKS

PUBLISHED BY W. S. JOHNSON, 60, SAINT MARTIN'S LANE, CHARING CROSS, LONDON.

The Home Circle is now Re-issued to enable New Subscribers to take this popular and useful Work from the commencement with greater facility. With the first number is presented, GRATIS, a magnificent large Steel Engraving, "SUNDAY EVENING."

In Weekly Nos., One Penny; Monthly Parts, 6d.; and Volumes, 4s. and 4s. 6d., gilt edges and back.

This is a Weekly Family Magazine of Literature, Science, Domestic Economy, Arts, Practical Information, Needlework, Chess, Knowledge, and Entertainment.

A work which may, without any fear of raising a blush, be placed in the hands of every member of a family, and which has been honoured by eulogiums from the entire Press of the United Kingdom, and those eminent Judges, BARON ALDERSON *and* SIR THOMAS NOON TALFOURD, KNIGHT.

———o———

The Ladies' Own Book, a Companion to the Work-Table, beautifully Illustrated with Original Designs, and containing elaborate instructions in every branch of Needlework.

Monthly Parts, Sixpence, and Half-yearly Volumes, 4s.

———o———

The Royal Dramatic Performances at Windsor Castle, elegantly bound, price £2 2s. (200 copies only printed,) the Complete Series of the Plays recently represented, by command, before Her Majesty the Queen, His Royal Highness Prince Albert, the Royal Family, and the Court, at Windsor Castle; with Illuminated Titles and Frontispiece in Colours, representing the Royal Audience in the Rubens' Gallery. The Plays printed verbatim from the authorized copies, with Fac-similes of the Bills of Performances.

———o———

A DISTINGUISHED STRANGER IN ENGLAND.

THE AMERICAN MAGAZINE, edited by "BROTHER JONATHAN." This Work is issued Monthly, and is designed as a medium of introducing the Works of the best American Writers only, to English firesides. In it will be found articles from the pens of FENIMORE COOPER, LONGFELLOW, WASHINGTON IRVING, CULLEN BRYANT, WALDO EMERSON, EDGAR A. POE, MRS. SIGOURNEY, MRS. CHILD, GRACE GREENWOOD, ETC., ETC. The floating wit, gossip, humour, and drollery of the American press is collected under the head of "Mosaic Work." Every Number contains a splendid Steel Engraving of some prominent view in the United States. The "American Magazine" will be found a brilliant, lively, chatty companion! Monthly, One Shilling.

———o———

In Ornamental Wrapper, 12mo., Price One Shilling.

The Young Chemist; or, Scientific Recreations. By HENRY HOWARD PAUL. A Book that should be in the hands of every youth in the land, containing several hundred pleasing and easy experiments.

Useful Items. Price SIXPENCE each, containing all the necessary information each subject can possibly require.

ETIQUETTE......How to conform to the Rules of Society.

THE COMPLEXION..How to Produce and Maintain a Clear White Skin.

THE TEETH......How to Preserve and Beautify.

THE HAIR ....How to Promote, Preserve, and Keep Luxuriant.

DRESS ....How to Adorn the Person.

THE DANCE......How to Behave in a Ball-room.

THE PARTY ......How to Arrange and Preside.

THE VISITOR ..How to Receive and Pay Visits:

COURTSHIP ......How to Woo and Win.

THE WEDDING ..How to Accomplish all its Arrangements.

THE HOUSEWIFE.How to Economize and Conduct a Home.

THE BABY ....How to Manage and Rear.

———o———

WORKS WRITTEN BY PIERCE EGAN,
EDITOR OF THE "HOME CIRCLE."

*Robin Hood and Little John; or, the Merry Men of Sherwood Forest. Super Royal 8vo., with 35 magnificent Wood Engravings, designed expressly for this edition, with a correct Likeness of the Author.
Weekly, ONE PENNY; Parts, SIXPENCE; One Volume, superbly bound.

*Wat Tyler, Super Royal 8vo., with 65 large Wood Engravings, drawn and executed by Artists of celebrity.
Weekly, ONE PENNY; Parts, SIXPENCE; One Volume, beautifully bound.

Quintin Matsys, the Blacksmith of Antwerp, Royal 8vo., elaborately illustrated with large Wood Engravings.
Weekly, ONE PENNY; Parts, FIVEPENCE; and in One Volume, elegantly bound.

London Apprentice and the Goldsmith's Daughter of West Chepe; or the Evil May Day; a Story of the Times of Bluff King Hal. Profusely illustrated by large Engravings.
Weekly, ONE PENNY; Parts, FIVEPENCE.

☞ *OBSERVE.—These Works are never out of Print. Back Numbers can always be had at the Office.*

* Be particular in asking for the Author's LARGE EDITION, published by W. S. JOHNSON.

———o———

The Witch of the Wave. Illustrated. The £50 Prize Novel. This startling Romance of the Sea will be found one of the most exciting works ever issued in a cheap form; it abounds in disasters by sea and land, perilous escapes, frightful explosions, and adventures with pirates: altogether a most remarkable work. Weekly Nos., One Penny; complete in Wrapper, One Shilling.

———————

CHILDREN'S SPELLING, STORY, NATURAL HISTORY, SONG BOOKS, &c.

Royal London Primer. Illustrated with 60 Wood Engravings, 36 pages in wrapper, 18mo. Twopence.

———

Large Penny 4to. Books, illustrated, colored and plain, in wrappers.

New London Alphabet. 52 Wood Engravings.

Parent's Best Gift for a Good Child. 17 Wood Engravings.

Royal London Primer. 25 Wood Engravings.

Jack the Giant Killer. 12 Wood Engravings.

Jack and the Bean Stalk. 12 Wood Engravings.

Old Mother Hubbard and her Wonderful Dog. 15 Wood Engravings.

Blue Beard, or Female Curiosity. 8 Wood Engravings.

Cinderella, or the Little Glass Slipper. 9 Wood Engravings.

Death and Burial of Cock Robin. 17 Wood Engravings.

www.ingramcontent.com/pod-product-compliance
Lightning Source LLC
Chambersburg PA
CBHW081214170626
46811CB00010B/3283